LIAM HOGAN is an award-winning short story writer, with stories in Best of British Science Fiction and Best of British Fantasy (NewCon Press), Analog, Nature Futures, BSFA Fission, and many more. He hosted the live literary event Liars' League for twelve years and remains a Liar. Liam also volunteers at the creative writing charities Ministry of Stories and Spark Young Writers.

He lives and writes in Shropshire. He does not have a dog.

Follow Liam on happyendingnotguaranteed.blogspot.co.uk

CW00820371

Praise for
A Short History of the Future

A SHORT HISTORY OF THE FUTURE

A COLLECTION OF 42 SCIENCE FICTION SHORT STORIES

LIAM HOGAN

NORTHODOX PRESS

Northodox Press Ltd
Maiden Greve, Malton,
North Yorkshire, YO17 7BE

This edition 2025

1
First published in Great Britain by
Northodox Press Ltd 2025

ISBN: 9781915179470

This book is set in Caslon Pro Std

CONTENTS

Chinese Fortune Cookie:

You are a lover of words,
and someday you will write a book.

INTRODUCTION

Ah, science fiction: the whiff of electricity, the flickering of strange lights, the faint echo of implausible explanations...

The boundaries between fantasy and science fiction have always been a little fuzzy. Time travel, of the sort that graces a fair few of these tales, is not science fiction. But it's how you do it that counts: is it via a time machine (borrowed, or otherwise), or is it by magic? And then there's whether or not you have to deal with the temporal consequences...

There's hard sci-fi, soft sci-fi, and yes, there's science-fantasy. You'll find all three in this collection. It's up to the reader to judge of the plausibility or otherwise of each piece, from the single photon of a micro-fiction, all the way up to the massive structures that keep black holes company. The question I concern myself with is, does it serve the story? In short, does it entertain?

I'll leave the answer up to you.

ANA

It's weird, the things that can mess up a kid's head. Take Ana, for example. She was convinced that every time she looked under her bed, the universe split in two. In a parallel world, in which a mirror version of Ana also looked under her bed before going to sleep and after saying her prayers and where, up until then, she'd never found anything bad, this time there would be a ghastly demon, with wicked teeth and blood-stained claws, whose only desire was to catch and tear apart Ana, aged six-and-three-quarter-years.

Little wonder she said her prayers *before* she looked. Little wonder she had nightmares.

I told her that wasn't the way multiverse theory worked. That for every Ana who found a slavering beast, there was one who found a toy she'd lost, or one who forgot to look under the bed.

She skewered me with her most outraged look. This Ana *never* forgot.

But it's hard arguing theoretical physics with a child yet to turn seven, and, as I wasn't prepared to deny the theory outright, it was clear this notion was not going to be an easy one to shift. It wasn't simply that she had a binary, yes versus no, either-or view of the coin toss that happened in her imagination every time she lifted the skirt that kept under-the-bed out-of-sight. It was because what terrified her wasn't the finding a monster under her bed, it was the *not* finding a monster under her bed. In her head, every time she survived, she doomed a parallel universe Ana to a grisly death. The guilt was crushing her.

'Why don't you not look?' I reasoned.

'I have to,' she replied with an air of ancient sorrow. 'There might be a monster under the bed. I have to check. And even if I don't, the other Ana will.'

This had me scratching my head, figuratively speaking. I'm a psychologist by trade, not a physicist. Wouldn't that require the universe to have already split? And, once the other Ana looked, it would be her universe that split again, not this Ana's. Maybe this was something I could use.

I thought of her parents. Reading between the lines, not a tricky task with those two, they wanted me to make Ana as easy to handle as she had been twelve months earlier. To make her 'normal'. But normal wasn't an option; it was clear this precocious child had the potential to far exceed the pretensions of her middle-class parents.

'Ana,' I said. 'Who looks first? You, or the other Ana?'

She suspected a trick and trod carefully. 'We both...' then she corrected herself. 'There is no other Ana, not until I look. Or there is, but it's me and we haven't split yet.'

'If she is you, will she react to finding the monster the same way you would?'

She sucked air through the gap in her front teeth. 'I guess.'

'And how would you react, if, when you looked under the bed, you found a monster there? What would you do?'

'I...'

I waited. The silence stretched between us. This was somewhere she hadn't been before. 'I don't know,' she said quietly.

'But you'd do something? You wouldn't just sit there?'

'No,' she agreed. 'I'd run. Scream, maybe.'

'I'm sure you would. And what would your parents do if they heard you scream?'

'They'd come running,' she said, and they would. Any parent would.

I let her think about this for a moment. 'Ana, you're intelligent, resourceful, and brave. And the other Ana, she is exactly the same. She is, after all, you. She - you - would not take it lying down. You'd fight, you'd run. Your parents would help. The one thing you would never be is a victim. Don't think I haven't noticed the hobby horse propped up against the toy chest, ready for action.'

'And the roller skates on the landing,' she said.

I wasn't sure how the roller skates would help. Perhaps she hoped the monster would trip on them. She'd be upset if I told her that her mother wordlessly tidied them up each night. 'And the skates,' I diplomatically agreed. 'It's not much, perhaps, but you're doing the best you can. And so would the other Ana. No monster is going to get a free lunch in this house.'

She laughed, a lovely little laugh, made all the more charming by its rarity of use.

I pushed on. 'So it's not a foregone conclusion that the monster always wins. And if it doesn't-'

'-Then there are two Anas!' she interrupted.

This wasn't quite where I'd been going. I wanted her to acknowledge that she wasn't responsible for what happened in the other universes. How could she be? But sometimes, usually in fact, you had to let your patient find their own path.

'And then four, and then eight, and then...' she babbled on.

A small chime rang out on my wristwatch. 'I think we've made good progress, Ana. We'll leave it there for today.'

A muffled voice came through the door. 'Ana? Honey? Who are you talking to in there?'

Ana called back, 'No one, mummy.'

Which was an illuminating denial. I jotted it down for future discussion, curious to see if Ana's mother would come into the bedroom. 'Okay, sweetie.' She caved in, as I suspected she would. 'But go to sleep now, you hear?'

Ana waited until the footsteps faded away down the hall. 'Goodnight, Doctor.'

'Goodnight, Ana,' I replied, 'sleep tight.'

And then I slid myself back under her bed, listening to her breathing softly slow and waiting for tomorrow night, when she would once again lift the covers, and - all being well - discover me lying there, ready for our next session.

ALL OUR FUTURES

All our futures arrived at once. Through a scorched sky, Morlocks flew anti-grav jetpacks above the ruins of a nanotec Statue of Liberty, aggressively buzzing the Apes, who returned potshots from phasers and plasma rifles as holographic adverts extolled the benefits of moving Off World.

As freezing flood waters swallowed spice worms and sentient robots defended their planet from invading Aliens beneath a swollen sun, I knew none of this was real. 'Last Orders at Milliways!' rang out over the distant echoes of trumpets as the stars went dark. After only the briefest of hesitations, I swallowed the red pill.

LIGHTER THAN AIR

The aliens never land until they're dead, and I'm about to find out why.

A-Gees, we call them. Some people think it stands for "Anti-Gravity", but that's wrong. It's "Aero-Gels". Their floating cloud-cities are built from a substance literally as light as air. They get their lift from school-bus sized cells of hydrogen gas. Cells that detach and drift between their cities, or that cluster together to form new clouds entirely.

They're here to save our planet.

The A-Gees are galactic *experts* at processing huge volumes of atmospheric gases. They filter *everything* they need from the air, to live, to build, to grow. Easy enough for them to get rid of what we *don't* need, in exchange for a new planet to co-habit.

But dropping their dried-out corpses like discarded litter was *not* part of the bargain.

'Dead weight,' is all they reply when our bureaucrats try to remonstrate with them. The A-Gees have a social media presence, have done from the start. Despite their growing numbers, almost six hundred cloud-cities by now, they're mostly silent. They listen but rarely respond, and then only in fragments of text no more substantial than their floating cities.

I suppose we don't entirely mind if they have to drop their dead to stay aloft. It's a small price to pay to fix our self-induced eco-disaster. But can't they do it somewhere *less* inconvenient? A tumble of dried skin and hollowed bones is not a good thing to have land on a kindergarten playground, even if it's far more likely to terrify than to actually hurt. The same for A-Gee corpses wedged on the glass roofs of shopping malls, until the winds get around to dispersing the feather-light fragments. Not fun to see, *even* at Halloween.

Can't the bodies be dumped over the oceans, we politely ask, or over forests, or at a pinch, over farmland?

But the A-Gees don't appear to understand. Any more than they understand international borders, flight corridors, or increasingly desperate attempts to compare or discuss or exchange technology. The A-Gees go where the winds take them.

Fortunately, a radar-reflecting cloud the size of a small town is not difficult to track; their drift not too difficult to predict. There haven't been any aircraft related accidents *yet*. And our government's renewed attempts to talk to the A-Gees have an unexpected result: I'm invited to go up and meet them. *Me*, Jess Silver, teenager, and vlogger!

Turns out the A-Gees are silent fans of 'Ag-Geek' or 'Silvergeek', as my stream is commonly known. They enjoy my nightly video pieces, my frothy mix of high school mini-dramas and musings on science and world - mainly climate-related - affairs.

All news to me as I'm dragged out of a drowsy Tuesday afternoon biology class, panicking about what I might have done, or worse; what terrible calamity has befallen my family, until the principal kindly puts me out of my misery. And, other than a pit-stop to get stunned parental permission and gather my video kit, I've been travelling ever since.

We're going up to meet the A-Gees at the oldest and largest of the cloud-cities, currently floating somewhere over the Mediterranean. A small committee of carefully selected diplomats, a handful of chew-their-own-legs-off-for-the-opportunity scientists. And, somehow, *I* get to tag along. Me! None of the big-wigs are happy I'm there. They make *that* abundantly clear, but my attendance is non-negotiable for the

A-Gees. If the big-wigs want a pow-wow, I'm along for the ride.

The final and scariest stage of my half-way round the world journey is by helicopter. A massive ex-military thing far too heavy to set down on a floating cloud, so we get to abseil to a jutting out platform where the A-Gees await. I'm delighted my braids and snug jumpsuit fare better than the uptight politicians' toupees and power suits and flappy ties. Score one to the vlogger.

But I *do* worry that I'll be stuck in boring meetings as policy advisors thrash out some mutually beneficial agreement, all while hoping to avoid an interstellar incident. The prospect almost makes double Math look attractive.

Thankfully (for the politicians as well as for me!) I'm not there for the negotiations. To the envy of the scientists, I'm getting a guided tour of this floating city. The first and only human to see behind the scenes. Silvergeek is going where no-one - well, no *human* - has gone before.

You've seen pictures of the A-Gees. Usually described as a half-starved pterosaur without the wings, as drawn by a not particularly talented third grader. Pictures don't do them justice. They might look like something out of a sci-fi show with a strong horror vibe, but my guide moves with an economy of effort that is shockingly graceful. I feel clumsy and slow and *heavy* in comparison. And I am; they've had to give me something like snowshoes to spread my load. Which isn't that much for a human, but here I weigh the same as a house! That's why the human visitors are always so carefully marshalled. The aero-gel walls are incredibly strong, but they're simply not designed for us. A diplomat going off-piste could end up doing serious damage, or worse; plummet through the fragile material to the earth far below.

In a half-dozen previous meetings between humans and A-Gees, the humans were herded between rooms created for the purpose, with strengthened floors and human-shaped furniture. By all accounts, the negotiations are tiresomely slow. Every so often, an A-Gee will get up "to consult with the ancestors", returning an hour later with either agreement or some new and unfathomable condition. Plenty of time for my tour.

'My name,' the guide says with something like a curtsey, 'is Li-La.'

'I'm Jess,' I say. I think about sticking out my hand, but decide not to. *Follow their lead* was the scientists' most helpful advice.

There's a small motion of her - or his - bird like head. 'I am aware. I watch on screen. Jess; one instruction please. *Observe. Listen.* Ask no questions.'

And that, I think to myself, is why I'm getting the grand tour and not one of the nosy exobiologists. Because the A-Gees are *people*, not exhibits in a zoo. We have no idea what taboos they have, what harm a casual query might cause. But they've twigged - no doubt through our social media - that there's a great deal of curiosity about them. Questions a vlogger may not answer, but I'll do my best.

So I do what they've asked of me, honoured and excited by the privilege. I *observe*. My shoulder cam a little ahead of me, one lens trained on my face, the other on what I'm seeing.

Instead of entering the meeting hall with the rest of the delegation, we head down steps no wider than my snowshoes. Cloudshoes? I take my time, unsure what would happen if I tumbled.

The bottom, widest layer of the city is where the air gets filtered, Li-La explains. What they don't use is expelled from the centre of the cloud and helps maintain altitude. It can even be directed, either to navigate or to counter light winds if they want to hover in place.

Li-La tells me what they mainly strip from the air is water. I'm handed a small cup to taste. It is cold and pure. Refreshing.

Like humans, A-Gees are mostly water, and like humans, it also forms the basis for much of their industry. But they're busy devouring everything *else* the air contains as well, including our unwanted pollutants.

Their aero-gels are carbon based. The A-Gees prefer to generate them from methane rather than carbon dioxide, which the earth scientists are more than happy about. Methane is a hundred times worse a greenhouse gas than CO_2, even if CO_2 sticks around for longer. A-Gees *love* methane. When weather conditions allow, they hover as close to its sources (swamps, rubbish dumps, warming tundra) as they can.

Eventually, they'll switch to harvesting the excess CO_2. The A-Gee-Human contract, their rights to colonise our skies, come in return for helping us achieve a reduction to three hundred parts per million, a level not seen for well over a century. We humans also have to go carbon neutral, of course, which we're still some way from managing. And that's why the scientists want to know how the A-Gees do what they do.

I doubt they'll get many clues from the video I'm streaming. There are no machines, no giant vats. I get the impression all their chemistry happens at some nano-level.

We return to where we started. Stood outside the opaque wall of the meeting room, hoping this is not the end of the tour, Li-La hands me a pair of goggles. When I slip them on I can *see* through the wall. See, in Technicolor hues, the humans and A-Gees gathered around the table beyond. There doesn't appear to be a lot of activity, so I suspect they're yet again waiting on some ancestor's advice. This respect is hard to reconcile with the casual treatment of the bodies of their dead. Though perhaps A-Gee souls are lighter than air. It wouldn't surprise me.

With a start, I realise this infrared shifted view is what A-Gees see all the time, or why else give me the goggles? They must have virtually no concept of privacy. As I turn my head away from the deliberations, I see movement all along this level; hundreds of A-Gees going about their daily business.

I glance down, but that turns out to be a bad mistake. The world spins far beneath me. Gingerly, I hand the goggles back. Li-La accepts them without a word.

We head up, the steps broader and shallower, the light brighter. The sunlit top of the cloud is where the hydrogen cells are stored. That's what all the water is for, Li-La explains. Photosynthesis. And despite the altitude, I haven't had any trouble breathing. The air must be rich with surplus oxygen.

We come to a spot at the very edge of the cloud. It's not for those with a fear of heights and I'm glad I'm no longer wearing the goggles. The bay I'm standing in is open to the elements and gently sloping, and I can't help hugging the wall, for fear of slipping. Li-La stands by my side, which makes me feel less like a scaredy-cat. It's a fabulous view, even so. Far below, the Mediterranean Sea sparkles. I can glimpse islands, ships, even another floating city nearby, a solitary cloud in an otherwise cloudless sky.

Odd to think it's a mere seven years since the deal was brokered by galactic powerhouse the Yrill, seven years since the first A-Gee city - *this* city - was delivered by one of their massive interstellars. How quickly the cloud-cities have spawned and spread!

Some conspiracy theorists claim we're being invaded by stealth, but it's hard to consider the A-Gees any sort of a threat. They don't seem very interested in what is happening below. Their technology lacks anything that resembles either weapons or defence. Besides, without them, emissions would still be rising, instead of finally showing signs of levelling off. By the time the A-Gees reach peak population, as agreed in the treaty at twelve thousand cloud-cities, our CO_2 levels will be in reverse, the climate disaster largely averted.

A single cell approaches as I'm staring out over rocky islands - somewhere near Greece? And then I realise the blimp is heading straight for us. It's not just a viewing gallery; it's a docking bay. Or perhaps, more simply, it's the *absence* of a hydrogen cell.

It's not clear why there is so much exchange between the floating cities, but such cells are always coming and going, whenever two cities are within a dozen miles of each other.

Perhaps they carry passengers?

I watch and so does my camera, as the cell fits itself to the waiting hole. There's a noise like mud sucking, a squelch of semi-transparent liquid that fills with fine snaking tendrils, knitting the edges together. Swiftly the cell is indistinguishable from all the others around us, our view gone as we stand in the corridor between.

'An ancestor wants to talk,' Li-La says, part of a wall shrinking away. I wait to see who or what emerges, but instead Li-La urges me forward.

Cautiously, I step through the oval doorway. There's no-one there, as the portal shrinks and vanishes. I wait. And *wait*. I think about switching the camera off to save power and to avoid boring my viewers. Finally, I sit.

'Jess Silver,' a quiet voice says. 'Thank you for coming. I very much enjoy your channel.'

I jerk back to standing, and the words fade.

They're coming from the floor. As well as, I realise, the walls, and even the ceiling.

I lie down again, resting my head on the soft pillow surface. And listen.

#

I never pay attention to the comments my video posts get. A schoolgirl fascinated by science is like a red rag to a troll and there are no shortage of haters. But when you're plastered across the newspapers or picked up on the evening news, it's harder to ignore.

There are different reports, different interpretations, of the recording I made. The voice I heard in my head - transmitted by vibrations of the floor? - does not show up on my shoulder cam. So it looks like I'm having a one-sided conversation with myself. Not much to watch, either; a featureless ceiling and me, blissed out, eyes alternatively wide or shut, lots of soft 'wow!'s and expressions of wordless wonder.

Some commentators say I must have been having a hallucinogenic trip, either because I'm a drug addled teenager, (as if!) or because the aliens spiked me, presumably with that cup of crystal-clear water. Others take it as evidence the whole A-Gee thing is an elaborate hoax (not elaborate enough to add a distorted soundtrack for the words of the aliens, though..?)

But, as I watch the video back, I can still mostly fill the silent gaps with what I was told up there in the artificial cloud. Not the exact words, but what I *learnt;* what I pieced together. I'm no scientist. I'll freely admit most of this is conjecture, pure and simple. But I think, I hope, I understand.

I've always loved butterflies.

The hydrogen cells, like the one I was in, *they're* A-Gees too. The whole city, from top to bottom, every wall, every corridor, *everything*, is A-Gees. Drones in a beehive. Each A-Gee has its job, its part of the whole, its role in the cloud.

The ones like Li-La, the ones the diplomats and scientists were talking to, they're the young. Adolescents. *Larva.* No wonder they nip off to consult with the ancestors whenever things get a bit tricky.

There must be a point in their life cycle when some of them start processing hydrogen. Perhaps based on gender, or maybe they're fed royal jelly. Who knows?

Whatever it is, before they can become lift-cells they have to shed their juvenile vestiges. *That* is what they jettison as 'dead weight'. Like the husk a butterfly leaves behind, it is nothing to them and our requests that they treat their dead with more respect are nonsensical.

The adult cells travel between cities not as sky-taxis, but because *they're* the leaders, the elders, the ones with the knowledge and experience. It's communication, or perhaps communion. And they can't provide samples, or swap tech, because there *is* no technology to share. It's all biology, all body chemistry. Somehow, the A-Gees can control their physical forms to do any number of tasks we have to build machines to do. Or maybe, like a jellyfish, they're not actually *one* species but many, living together for a common purpose.

Mr Franklin's biology lessons have come in handy after all. Because if nothing else, they've told me how *weird* life on earth is. Surely, we have to expect alien life to be even weirder.

The aliens don't want to explain themselves to us because we couldn't possibly understand. All they want is for us not to worry. All they want is to be left alone.

I wonder what happens after the A-Gees have lowered the methane and CO_2? When we're not so dependent on each other. Will we still be able to coexist peacefully?

I sincerely hope so. It was beautiful up there. Sometimes I dream of flying. I suppose we all do. Only now I actually think of it, it was never flying - it was floating.

#

Before I leave, I take one last look at the bright canopy above me. The roof of the cell I've been listening to contains a multitude of much smaller cells, some darker than others.

Are these... *baby* A-Gees? There's at least a hundred of them, maybe a thousand. No wonder the cloud-cities proliferate so fast.

No wonder the A-Gees are peaceful. Or probably, *hopefully* so. When every wall, every staircase is sentient, their weapons would be completely unlike anything we use. No guns, knives, or explosives. If they have anything at all, I bet we have no defence against it, just as A-Gees would have no defence against tracer fire and air-to-air missiles.

If we ever fought, we'd end up waging two totally different wars, winning one, losing the other. Best not go there.

These thoughts keep me subdued as Li-La guides me down. The meeting below is coming to an end, the helicopter on its way to pick us up. From the grim faces of the politicians, little if anything was resolved.

But that's *ok*, I think. Whatever the A-Gees do, we'll just have to get used to them. We've gotten used to far worse.

I wonder if the Yrill know anyone who could clean up our oceans?

STARBORN, STARBIRTH

The tired old star burns fat and hot and slow. Now, as the end approaches, firestorms flicker and die and are born anew across its roiling surface. At its core, helium ashes are squeezed and the heat there builds and builds, stuttering with the idea of something new. Now, we detach ourselves from the fields in which we have gambolled for countless aeons, where we have long feasted and bred. Diving deep in our displays of courtship, kicking up great tendrils of supercharged plasma through which to leap and skip and dance, filtering out the heavier elements as we do. Now, we drift outwards, cooling rapidly in the hostile vacuum, hardening our hearts as we majestically unfurl our vast, fragile wings. Gossamer thin, we float past rocky planets, long stripped of their seas, their delicate atmospheres, whose once molten centres are frozen and still. There was life here, we are amused to note. Brief, faltering life, as ethereal as the waves from a solar flare, as short-lived as our mating songs.

And on we riders go, to the next planet, the next barren rock. Life fled here when its cradle had grown too warm, too polluted. A brief respite only, a staging ground for the next faltering step. And on again we and the echoes of it drift, past the remnants from the solar system's ancient creation to the next planet, to the moons that circle like clockwork around the gassy giant, itself too small to ignite, too cold to offer us sustenance. Though a few of us try anyway and are quickly swallowed by its dense, unpalatable clouds, wings ripped away and for a moment flaring bright, the imprint swiftly forgotten.

The giant, and its lesser gas-planet neighbour, will feed the inferno that is yet to come. The shock-wave might perhaps briefly fire them into life, before stripping their clouds, leaving them stunned and stunted in the dimming afterglow, finally exposing what the dense atmosphere conceals.

We wonder whether the life that is not our life ever attempted to escape this far. There are no signs in the cold, outer fringes. Perhaps it went further still; daring the void between the stars as we too are about to do, in search of new planets to taint. Perhaps we will catch up with them as we journey beyond the point where the solar wind is snuffed out by the much softer, but more extensive, interstellar medium. Beyond the insubstantial border where you could truly be said to have shed the bounds of the star that even now is just a baleful, fat, reddened point. Perhaps. But there is no hurry.

Looking back, we watch as our brethren gather, our number too numerous to count. There is a sweet-spot, a place we all hope to be when the moment comes. Some will time it wrong; they always do. They will fill their bellies a little too full, rise a little too slow, too late, engorged and still soft and fragile, their wings only partially unfurled when the cataclysm comes.

Others have left too early. Millions or even billions of years too early, tired perhaps of waiting. They haven't got very far, and they will be cold and perhaps dead by now. Pushed only by the last beats of a burning heart, slumbering for an eternity, dreaming of what might have been.

This too is the way.

Only a few of us, a handful of the myriad, will fall upon more fertile ground, many millennia from now. But all of us will ride the death of the star we grew up on, letting its final, dying light push us out into the unexplored galaxy, looking for new homes, new stars, new life.

Rarer still, perhaps only one in a generation, one rider might find themselves not captured by another star, but surrounded by a veil of interstellar gases instead. With their wings stretched so thin it will be as though they're not there, they will begin to turn, the steady rhythm creating eddies and gathering in more and more of the tantalising dust, feeding an aeon-old hunger. Only one will sing the song of becoming as she slowly retracts her wings, cloaking herself within the thickening hydrogen cloud, spinning faster and faster and faster until, the cosmos be willing, she gives birth to a brand-new star.

THE BETSEY

Much as I loved the Old Girl, I was mighty glad when we finally hove into the space port at Sigma Draconis. It had been a long journey. Eleven years, relativistic, and even though I and the rest of the crew had deep-slept most of the way, this was no Rip-Van-Winkle trip. The *Betsey Trotwood* was imbued with a first-generation Ship AI and the engineers never fully trusted Her, so they built in an optical drive. In other words, Ship was blind, unless a human operator was peering into the scope on the bridge.

We took it in turns: three of the thirteen-man crew awake at any one time, one of those three on Watch; shifts within shifts. Our eleven-year run had cost me and everyone else aboard around two and a half years, biological. We were overdue some Ship leave.

Modern cargo crews have it easy, deep sleeping from space port to space port, granting full operational control to their more advanced AIs for everything but the loading and unloading. Might as well have no human crew on board at all; a step penny-pinching shipping companies were sure to take, eventually. The thought gave me the creeps. But, other than a few unsubstantiated rumours, no AI Ships had (to my knowledge) ever gone fully rogue.

As the *Betsey*'s engines became conspicuous by their unaccustomed absence, I rested my hand on the shoulder of the Watch. 'Stand down, Symons.'

She broke contact and looked at me askance, one eye reddened and ringed by the mark of the scope's suction cup. 'It's Fuller, sir. Cerys Fuller?'

I cursed under my breath and gave her an apologetic smile. I like to think I'm a pretty good Captain, but I always was lousy with names. It didn't help that there were a crowd of them to remember. By now, the full Ship's complement was awake, milling around and getting kind of fidgety. It was my job to calm them down.

'Patience, everyone,' I told them. 'You all know how long docking procedures can take. And stay focused: we've had a smooth journey this far. I'd like that to continue until I have the first beer in my hand.'

There was a cheer, in part because tradition dictated that, once on-shore, I'd be standing them all a drink. Ship was dry, of course; being light years away from help and drunk in charge of a four-thousand tonne, fusion powered cargo vessel was not generally considered a great combination. But, despite their obvious impatience, my crew was quickly back at their posts, running system checks and... well, basically waiting.

We waited an *awfully* long time.

When the umbilical dock finally blinked green and the iris-door smoothly opened, I wasn't surprised to see an official-looking chap floating there, slowly turning green. There would, no doubt, be a number of hoops to jump through before we disembarked; a few palms to grease. All through the bulging purse of the parent company, of course. This trip the *Betsey* was flying under the HianJin Shipping flag.

That the official was flanked by a couple of beefy looking guards... well. That wasn't all that unusual either. It was why I greeted them alone, as Captain, even while the rest of the crew listened, crammed into the adjacent mess hall. We were guests at the space port and sometimes they liked to flex their bureaucratic muscles before allowing us to cross the threshold.

I was, however, surprised, and somewhat bemused to see the state of the curved docking corridor stretched out beyond them; wires drifted loose from detached maintenance panels, a couple of bulkhead lights out or on the fritz. Given such units are usually rated for around fifty years' use, that gave the passageway a doleful air of long neglect. It certainly wasn't the entry to the vibrant main hub I remembered from my previous visits; the crews of a dozen ships swapping news and renewing acquaintances beneath brightly coloured advertising as they readjusted to the artificial gravity, to the hubbub of an exotic cluster of food and drink concessions.

Perhaps the hub was overcrowded, I reasoned. But I already knew which other Ships were currently docked. The space station was some ways from full capacity. Still. Best not to jump to hasty conclusions. No doubt the queasy looking gravity-hound would enlighten me.

'Captain Jay D'Red,' I smiled, and gave a small bow, 'Are you Customs or..?'

'Legal,' the official snapped in reply. He reached out, but not to shake; depositing his flimsy in my outstretched hand instead. I took it and tapped it against the one clipped to my belt before handing it back, but I didn't do more than glance at the transferred copy. It looked long and wordy. I returned my questioning gaze to the man before me.

He sighed and shuck his head, as if my failure to instantly take in the full ramifications of the tome he'd delivered was a personal affront.

'The CSS *Betsey Trotwood* is hereby impounded,' he intoned, his eyes flicking everywhere but on mine. 'Permission for the crew to disembark will not be given. Permission for the Ship to depart will not be given. Do-Not-Depart clamps have been engaged. You are to remain at this docking bay until further notice. Good day!'

My smile faltered as he turned to go. 'Wait, please. What's all this about? And I... I don't believe I got your name?'

'It's all in the documents.' He sniffed, and then seemed to relent a little. 'It's *Starr*; Harold Starr. As an attorney, I represent the creditors for the collapsed HianJin Shipping company.'

'Collapsed?'

'Bankrupt, Mr D'Red. For two years now.'

'Ah, I see.' I nodded as if indeed I did see. I hadn't thought it possible for a Space Shipping company to fold, not in this day and age, with more and more destinations opening up and the galactic economy positively booming. Assuming it was still booming? Might it have collapsed over the eleven years since our Earth departure? But there were a couple of high-end luxury cruise Ships docked at the space port and tourism was usually the first victim of a financial slump. My nod turned into an uncertain shake.

Time was, the only thing we moved around was data. We still did, mainly. It's more efficient to transfer scientific information by spaceship than to beam it across the light years, even if you did have to wait a little longer for the delivery. A detailed planetary survey was worth its weight in reactor grade tritium and intergalactic bandwidth was slow, massively inefficient, and horrendously error prone.

It was only in the last century or so that we'd started delivering luxury goods to the galaxy's best and brightest. In the *Betsey*'s hold was such a load; two dozen autonomous humanoid droids, top of the range, Earth's finest robotic creations.

Thinking of them, I stopped Mr Starr once more. 'What about the cargo?' I asked, 'Surely the buyers want their goods?'

His lips pursed together again. 'Actually, no.' He handed back his flimsy, but this time I didn't bother to transfer the contents to mine. It showed a glossy brochure from the Osiris Robotics Company. A sleek, gleaming plexi-skin face stared out at me like something from a Sci-Fi holo-movie. The specs were even more impressive: stronger, faster, more intelligent, wipe clean and with vastly improved battery life. It appeared ORCs had come a long way in a scant dozen years.

'What's this?' I pointed, 'Programmed with full obedience to the three laws of Robotics?'

'New feature.' He nodded. 'Totally, infallibly, safe. Owners no longer need full liability cover.'

I whistled low. 'The TX-R3000's are obsolete?'

'So it would appear. The owners are happy to let the insurance company cover their losses, even if it means they'll be waiting another nine years for their replacements.'

'And... so what happens to my cargo?'

He shrugged. 'I expect they'll be scrapped for parts. As will the Ship.'

'The *Betsey*? Scrapped? You can't be serious!'

I could hear the angry murmur of voices from the mess hall next door and coughed until it ebbed away.

'How old is this ship, Mr D'Red?' the ferret-faced lawyer asked, once I'd recovered from my 'fit".

I had to think for a moment. I'd been on the *Betsey* almost a hundred and twenty years, a quarter of that awake. The *Betsey* was as much home for me as anywhere was. With my years spent in time-defying torpor, we were roughly the same age, She and I, even if my biological clock only said fifty-five.

'A hundred and forty-three, operational; a hundred and eighty-two years, Solbased. Well beyond the normal operational limit,' Starr answered for me, shaking his head. 'Nobody wants an optical drive any more, Mr D'Red. Even with a complete systems overhaul, the *Betsey Trotwood* would still be a clunking antique. Why, you should see some of the new Ships that come in to Sigma Draconis! Nano-tech infrastructure, giving an infinitely flexible hold space. Astounding.' He gave me a small but undeniably pitying smile. 'I'll be in touch about arrangements. Good day.'

The docking portal shushed closed, displaying a 'NOT to be opened without Space Port Authorisation!' warning. I slowly made my way to the messhall, to speak with the crew.

#

Fuller looked sheepish as she slung her kit bag over her shoulder.

'I'm sorry, Captain. But... you understand?'

I did. I understood and I can't say I blamed them. Most of the crew were single. Heck, most of them were orphans. No family, no connections. Connections don't survive the years, or the light-years, for that matter. But that doesn't stop them wanting to settle down, eventually. Crewing the spacelines was a means to an end, a way of earning enough to set themselves up for life, wherever and doing whatever they wanted, be it a pig farmer on the moons of Sorastro; hover engineer on Calypon 5; or even heading Sol-bound, living out the rest of their lives on some crowded hippy heat-commune.

After two long months of twiddling their thumbs, wasting away their days, surviving on basic rations, Starr had offered them the choice of staying on an impounded, overcrowded, clamped *Betsey*, in legal-limbo with no end in sight, *or* signing away all their rights to any back-pay and seeking gainful employment elsewhere. Well. *Sure,* I understood.

It might not have been so bad if we'd known it would take this long from the start. Half the crew or more could have slept it out, leaving room for the rest of us. Heck, we all could have slept; the Ship wasn't going anywhere.

But the legal resolution was always 'just' round the corner, as, of course, was the promise of that first beer. I should have known better. We'd be stuck here for as long as it took for a final settlement of the HianJin affairs, and maybe another half-dozen years after that for news of that settlement to filter through to Sigma Draconis. The lawyers would be picking over the bones for a good decade yet. I wondered how many other Ships were in the same sorry, becalmed state.

Waiting, waiting, waiting, and all to end up - if they were as old as the *Betsey* - as mere parts and scrap metal.

So yeah, and again *yeah,* I understood why my crew was leaving the sinking Ship. It was their livelihoods, their futures, that were at risk. It was a good crew. They'd do all right, despite the loss of earnings from this trip. Maybe they'd even get a job aboard one of those moving-wall nano-Ships.

Of course, the same offer wasn't open to me, and I wouldn't have taken it if it were. I was the Captain; the *Betsey* was my Ship, whatever it said on the legal paperwork. I'd worked my way up through the ranks, sat the exams, put in the runs. Tackled the head-twisting mathematics of rudimentary astronavigation, even if Ship managed that well enough itself. Got the painful throat implant that allowed sub-vocal communication, even in the case of explosive decompression. Kept on working long after my contemporaries had retired to fritter away their savings, until, finally, I'd been given my command, and the *Betsey*. It was all I'd ever really wanted, though it had taken the best part of my life to achieve it. Maybe we *were* past it, she and I, but still, I wasn't ready to retire and nor was the Old Girl.

As the men and women of my crew filed through into the fading space port corridor, heads bowed, stubbornly not looking back to where I stood, as they pressed their flimsies against the lawyer's forms, I had a sudden overwhelming sense of the empty space at my back, of aching solitude, and of loss.

The portal spun resolutely shut, and the minutes ticked away as I continued to stare at it, trying to navigate a path to the future in the maelstrom of my thoughts. Finally, I turned away from that damned warning message and towards the silent corridors of the *Betsey*.

'Ship,' I said and felt the reassuring tickle at the back of my throat that meant She was listening. 'We're going to need a new crew.'

#

'Well?' snapped Mr Starr, talking even before the portal was fully open. 'I'm a busy man, Mr D'Red. What did you drag me out here for? Very important, you said. Of legal significance.

Well? What is it?'

'If you'll accompany me to the cargo bay, all will become clear,' I replied, but he didn't move for a moment, staring at me instead.

'What on Sol have you done to your face?' he gurgled.

I tapped the hastily improvised eye patch and shrugged, then gestured with my hand, beckoning him to follow, turning away from his half-horrified, half-bewildered look. I heard him mutter as he trailed behind me, clumsy in zero-g.

In the cargo hold, twenty-three and a half robots stood, silent and inert.

'So?' the Lawyer exclaimed, when he saw them. 'Unpacking - even dismantling - these obsolete robots won't change how fast the legal status of the *Betsey* is resolved, Mr D'Red, as well you know.'

He pointed to the head on the work bench, wires dangling from an empty eye socket. 'And if you've damaged them in any way, if you've lowered their scrap value, you'll find yourself financially responsible for the loss!'

There was a sudden lurch as the *Betsey*'s powerful engines started up, a distant alarm as the space port umbilical desperately tried to close and undock at the same time. Mr Starr's look changed from petulant anger to confusion, and then to horror, his face pale and drawn. 'How..? We're clamped!'

'Not any more,' I said, as the lawyer's voice echoed from the internal speakers, repeating the orders she'd just given the space port. 'This is Mr Starr authorising a test drive of the impounded *Betsey Trotwood*. Please release docking clamps. Authorisation code P-R-I-M-Zero.'

'Turns out Ship does a decent line in mimicry,' I grinned.

He shook his head. 'You are in SO much trouble, Mr D'Red! Faking legal authorisation, impersonating an accredited Lawyer, ignoring docking protocols, risking health and... and...'

Realisation dawned. 'But you're the only crew member on board! Who's on Watch?'

'I am,' I said, lifting my eye patch, exposing the plugged-in circuitry as the last of the colour drained from the Lawyer's face. The robot eye was effectively turned the wrong way round, so it must have all looked a bit ghastly. It didn't let me see, exactly. Rather, it transmitted what my eye was seeing back to me. My real eye, the one floating in nutrient gel and attached to the Ship's Optical Drive. A split view: that which was in front of me and that which the *Betsey* saw through her external monitors, all glittering stars and a shrinking space port still venting debris from the old docking area. It took some getting used to. But I supposed I'd manage.

'What in hell!' he spluttered. 'Do you seriously believe taking me hostage will solve *anything*?'

'Oh, I haven't taken you hostage, Mr Starr. I only needed you on board to release the clamps before I could depart. You're free to go.'

On cue, one of the activated TX-R's grabbed him by the arms. He struggled and swore, and said all manner of ungentlemanly, unlawyerly, things. He really was rather slow on the uptake.

I didn't actually make him "walk the plank", of course. That was just my little joke, though I don't think he found it funny. I merely had the TX-R escort him into one of the *Betsey*'s escape pods. I'd thought of sending it and him out in a wide hyperbolic orbit, taking the same three months he'd kept us unnecessarily waiting. But frankly, I didn't want to waste Ship's rations on him. A quarter-speed drift would have him back at the space port safe and sound in, oh, a Sol day or two. Sooner if anyone bothered coming to retrieve him. But I guessed my sudden departure might give them other things to worry about for a while.

I turned to the rest of the waiting droids. 'TX-R3005... or are you 3008?' I peered at the badge on the nearest forehead, squinting at the tiny writing. I don't think the Osiris Company ever considered that anybody might need more than one of their androids. As it was, I was faced with a crew twice as large and many times more difficult to identify than when I'd had a normal human crew.

'Hell blast it,' I sighed in exasperation, before brightening up. Who said they had to be treated as individuals? They were all linked to the Ship, and therefore, via my implant, to me. 'TX-R3000s, hear this: I shall henceforth refer to all of you as 'R'. Divide my orders between you in the most efficient manner.'

Twenty-three TX-R3000's smartly replied: 'Yes, Captain'.

The disembodied head of the twenty-fourth rolled its one good eye at me from the workbench, the effects of my extreme tampering messing with its sophisticated programming. 'Arr!' it parroted, the voice higher pitched and softer due to the lack of an echo-chamber.

Maybe it wasn't *totally* unsalvageable after all.

I picked the head up. It lolled a little on what was left of its neck stalk before the wandering eye snapped into focus.

'So,' I asked it, 'What shall we do with an ageing, overpowered, renegade interstellar cargo ship, and two dozen almost top-of-the range, vacuum enabled, semi-indestructible metal men, hmm?'

#

The sleek tourist vessel, backlit by the gloriously ringed outer planet, filled the view from my Watch eye. That was the beauty of Sigma Draconis, a system of three habitable planets and a dozen mining and research stations. Cruise liners and supply ships ran back and forth like a trail of plump ants. And, what with the Krillian wars eternally simmering at the fringes of the human sector, there wasn't a military vessel for nigh on fifty light-years in any direction.

'Sir, the *Princess Royale* is in range,' one of my crew reported.

'Hail her and put her up on the monitor,' I ordered. 'All Rs, prepare for EVA.'

A boyish face appeared on screen, squinting. I knew he could only just about see me in the subdued light, but I didn't want to spoil the surprise.

'This is Ensign Choy, of the pleasure ship the *Princess Royale*. We're not expecting a rendezvous. Also, your Ship flag appears to be malfunctioning. Please confirm identity?'

'Jolly Roger!' squawked a feeble voice. 'Skull and Crossbones!'

'Say again, Ship, you're coming across distorted?' the Ensign said, as I cursed and sub-vocalised a 'Hush!' command.

'Apologies, *Princess*,' I said, reading the cruise Ship's cargo manifest. Really, electronic identification flags made it far too easy. My lips smacked as I scanned the list of luxury foods and, even better, beverages. Rum appeared to be the one thing that made my split vision relatively painless. 'This is the, um, CSS *Roger Jolie*. We may have taken a micro-meteorite to our flag.'

'Uh-huh.' The Ensign looked doubtful, as well he might. The 'flag' also housed the Ship's black box recorder and was, in theory, the most shielded part of the whole vessel. Still, it was *technically* possible. 'And your purpose?'

'Plunder!' the voice at my shoulder whispered. It appeared my command had not shut it up, just lowered its volume. I ignored it, hoping the Ensign would do the same.

'Tell me, *Princess,* with over a hundred passengers on board and *wow*, a really quite generous quantity of all-inclusive alcohol, I guess some of your crew are trained in unarmed combat skills? For peace-keeping purposes?'

'Well yes, but-'

'And no doubt there are even a number of small calibre firearms in the Captain's locker?'

'I'm sorry, Sir, I'm not at liberty-'

'And is there anybody on board handy with a cutlass, or who can at least fence?'

'Cutlass? I, um...'

No, of course there was no-one handy with a cutlass. But

that was all for the good. Because there's nothing to quell a have-a-go hero quite like a metal-shielded, bullet-immune, space-breathing, super-strong automaton. Especially one who *was* armed with a wickedly sharp sword, re-purposed from tungsten-steel K-cables. One tiny nick of their space suit and your hero had a whole ton of other things to worry about, like making it to the nearest airlock, ASAP. I'd have a nice, quiet, docile Ship to loot. Which was for their sake, not mine. Heck, I was doing them a service. Think of the story they'd live to tell their grandchildren!

In my Watch eye, a cloud of glinting figures swarmed through the hard vacuum towards their target. I'd kept him talking long enough.

'Ah, well that *is* a shame,' I said, with a grin. 'And now, kind sir, if you'll take a look in your external monitors, you'll notice you have company. Prepare to be boarded!'

'Board!' agreed Polly, the one android I'd bothered to name, as its head, mounted on my shoulder, rocked forward and into the Ensign's view, the glittering eye patch matching mine.

'But, but...' the Ensign quivered, face agog, torn between what was on screen and the whole host of alarms beginning to sound around him. 'Who are you? And - what - *are* they?'

'Who are we?' I laughed, 'Have you not heard? Why, we're the Jay D'Red Space Pirate Robots!'

'Arr!' echoed Polly, metal face contorted into a demonic and lopsided leer. 'Dread Pirate Robots!'

It has a certain ring to it, don't you think?

STAR LITTLE, TWINKLE, TWINKLE

They say time's arrow points both ways...

But as I stare up at the night sky, what are the odds?

Of a photon leaving my eye,
        travelling light years out into the cosmos,
              and colliding with a waiting star?

The "What-The" Tree

I lurch upwards, fighting to gulp air, my body trying to remember how. A pressure on my chest prevents me from flying off.

'Breathe,' a distant voice commands, and I do.

A warm flannel is passed roughly over my preservative-numbed and gunk-covered face as the tank drains around me, the vacuum pumps gurgling as the last of the fluid is sucked away. If anything, the air feels even colder than the liquid. Slowly, painfully, I crack open my eyes, light flaring across them.

The room is quiet, the bays to either side dark and empty, as unlike the organised chaos of our departure as anything can be. Am I the last to be awakened or the first?

I peer through a blurry film and keep blinking until it clears. An unnaturally slim girl with close-cropped hair, wearing a plain, grey jumpsuit, rests upside down on the wall above me. That is, if there *is* an 'above' or a right way up, which is pretty debatable in zero-G.

'Hi,' she says, her voice muffled by something going pop in my ears, 'I'm uh, Stella.'

I burp and a small glob of congealed substance breaks off and floats embarrassingly towards the impish young woman, perched like a gargoyle in the corner of the room. I think about making some quip about stumbling over or forgetting your own name, but my brain feels like it's been mashed, and I can't think of anything worth the effort.

'Are we there?' I croak instead.

She pouts. 'Well, and 'hello' back. 'Nice to meet you too' and a hearty 'Thanks!' for bringing me back to life.'

I venture a smile, though I've no idea if the result is even in the right ballpark.

'I wasn't dead,' I point out. 'I was sleeping.'

'Yeah?' she says, her head rocking back. 'Had any good dreams lately?'

Of course I haven't had any dreams; no-one does. But this spacer is on the prickly side of the spectrum. And I thought I was the one who got out on the wrong side of deep sleep. Or maybe it's the same mordant wit that has spacers calling their passengers 'corpses' and the wake-up area 'the resurrection room'.

I spread my hands in what I hope is a placating manner. 'Alright, alright. Thank you, Stella-'

'Not *Stella*, Mr. Third-Rating Xenobiologist *Brad*-ley Harrison. *E*-stella. Got it?'

I nod, swallowing to clear my ears that had confused an *uh* with an *E*, then wonder what the heck I'm swallowing.

She watches me grimace and shrugs away her scowl. 'As to whether we're there yet, depends where you mean by '*there*'. Come on, get yourself cleaned and dressed. I've got something to show you.'

I look down at my shivering, near naked body, my fingers and toes wrinkled and blue, the scrap of sodden fabric at my waist the only thing protecting my modesty. 'Some privacy, please?'

She laughs. 'On a spaceship?' She holds my gaze for a whole minute and then turns abruptly away. I had the best teachers at the Academy: dry academics always trying to push your buttons, waiting for you to give a hasty or ill-thought reply, hoping to get you canned. No spacer is going to outstare *me*.

She kicks off from the wall, executing a perfect somersault as she flies towards the door, launching a thin towel in my direction on the way. 'Clean jumpsuits under the medi-bay. You're probably - nah, *definitely* - a small. Don't keep me waiting, Mr. Third-Rating.'

She's loitering in the corridor outside when I clumsily emerge. 'We're not at Perseus 3, are we?' I ask, rubbing my elbow where I'd banged it on the door frame. A day's worth of zero-G training wasn't nearly enough for the tight confines of this ship, though by all accounts most colonists don't get even that much.

She shakes her head. 'No, Bradley, we're not. And you're the only cargo we've awakened. I've got the job of showing you where we are and why.'

She goes slowly but still has to wait at each junction for me to catch up. 'See the loops?' she says, pointing at what, at that moment, was the floor for me, the ceiling for her. 'You can use them for more than just pushing against. Stick your hand in one at a junction and you can change direction as well. Only don't push too hard - we don't want any broken wrists.'

She moves like a fish underwater, effortlessly, gracefully. I move like a drunken hippo. I wonder for a moment if, were I to share that thought, she'd know what a hippo was. Probably not.

'How old are you, Estella?' I ask as she waits impatiently at yet another junction. The space tug *Vesta* is larger than I'd thought, and emptier; we've not seen anyone else on it.

'Just because we're on first-name terms already, Bradley, that don't give you the right to ask a lady's age. Anyhow, which age are you interested in? Earth? Biological? Elapsed?'

'Um, any of them? All of them,' I say, ready to dredge up whatever physics lectures I could remember: time dilation, deep sleep ratios, and the like.

'Hmm.' She thinks for a second, briefly allowing me to catch up before gliding on to the next intersection. 'Well, we're roughly the same biological age, I guess, both 17. Lived, I'm older by a couple of months, since I haven't spent any of *my* life as a corpse. Earthwise, there you have the seniority, having been in the tanks five years. Don't count for nothing, though, Earth age. It's experience that matters.'

I probably look as confused as I feel. Only five years into a seventy-something-year flight? Also, how come *she* hasn't been asleep? Then something clicks – she's a spacer child. You don't put a juvenile in the tanks; it messes with their development. She must have been twelve and still growing when the mission began, catching up with my biological age while I did a Rip Van Winkle impression, the low temperatures of deep sleep turning her half-decade into my half-year. Poor kid. I dread to think what life on the *Vesta* must have been like with no one your age around, and almost everyone asleep.

None of which explains what I'm doing awake – what *anyone* is doing awake – when we should be speeding through empty space, the gentle impulse of *Vesta's* mighty engines tugging the *Electryon* towards a decent fraction of light speed.

I notice she hasn't mentioned any relativistic effects, so I guess we're still travelling at a snail's pace. I wonder if she'd get *that* reference?

'Here we are,' she says as the corridor opens up. 'The lookout.'

'O-K...' I say. 'Are you going to raise the shields? My X-ray vision isn't quite up to the task.'

She rests a nail-bitten finger on the control. 'Promise you won't freak out?'

'Promise,' I say, wondering what I'm about to not freak out about. I know I won't be seeing Perseus, not as anything other than a bright speck still many more light years away than I'd hoped. The Earth, maybe. Perhaps we've been turned around for some reason and I'm about to be given a chance to abort my part in this colony mission.

That would be some decision to make. Right up until the final briefing, I'd have known exactly what my answer would be. Though now I'm not so sure. It must be that then: the Earth. What else could it be?

What else indeed.

'What the..?' I gasp and fall silent, the words sucked into the void before me.

Estella giggles. 'You owe me!' she says. 'I bet the Captain a week's cleaning duty you'd say that! Isn't it the most beautiful..?'

My hearing goes all tinny and Estella fades into background noise. I'd grab hold of something to stop me falling, except there's nowhere to fall and nothing but a gamine spacer to grab onto. I blink my eyes, certain for a moment that this is some sort of after-effect of hibernation, some optical illusion.

But it's not. It's a real, honest-to-god black hole, up close and extremely personal. For a moment I feel like I'm being pulled towards the three-inch-thick viewing window, but I know that's just my head messing with me.

I've seen pictures of black holes before, or at least computer simulations. Enough to know that, from an observer's viewpoint, they're very rarely black. Anything that gets sucked in spends a lot of time shedding gravitational energy; accretion disks and swirling clouds of dust heating up and radiating fiercely in the infrared; strange effects like Masers beaming brightly away; eddies glowing wherever the plasma is stretched or pinched; and narrow jets precessing around the spinning poles. I never expected to be this close to one and that alone would have been enough to take my breath away.

But I'm not staring at the black hole. I'm staring at something no simulation ever has or ever could depict.

Overlaid against the already spectacular view is a crown of black thorns, a webbed cradle, thick and knotted in some places, but in most a barely-visible thinness of dark spun silk. A gigantic, arced limb stretches before us, bent like a taut bow, reaching far into the distance. On the near, free end of it, lurking at the edge of the Vesta's viewing screen, is a rough-hewn sphere, black against the turbulent cloud beyond, which glows and sparks, sending glints of stellar fire licking over the sphere's surface.

Estella has been babbling all along, but I haven't heard a word. I interrupt her mid-flow: 'What the hell... is that?' My voice comes out husky, alien, as though from somewhere else altogether.

She pouts again. 'I thought I'd been explaining...' She trails off, searches my bewildered eyes. 'I'll start again, shall I?'

She reaches out a hand and takes mine, grips it firmly, a warm dryness against my clammy cold.

'We call it a black hole tree. Or just a What-The... tree. It's mostly iron and heavier metals, with a sprinkling of ice and organic compounds. It collects what it needs to grow from the dust that falls past and uses what it doesn't - vast quantities of hydrogen - to maintain its orbit. And, yes, under pretty much anyone's definition, it *has* to be considered alive.'

'What is it... *doing* here?' I manage to say.

'Like I said, they live around black holes. It's a black hole tree?'

I shake my head, trying to organise my thoughts. There's only one black hole in spitting distance of Earth and I might not know much in the ways of astronavigation, but it certainly isn't en route to Perseus. 'What are *we* doing here?'

'Hitching a lift.' She smiles. 'All that stuff they teach you about space travel...did you never stop to do the math? You really think plasma wakefield reactors could get us there? Carrying the reaction mass we need to slow down again at the other end? Carrying a great lummox of a colony ship? We've burnt everything we had in our tanks getting here and only managed a pitiful two-and-a-bit percent of light speed before reversing thrust. At that rate, we'd take - oh, something like five hundred years to get to Perseus. Whereas-' She points towards the sphere at the periphery of the view screen. '-See the dirty great blob on the end of the arm? That's our ride. Every manned interstellar journey ever made has been made in one of them. We hollow out a nice cavity, slide in the *Vesta* and your bloated colony ship, then we sit tight and wait.'

'Wait? For how long? And for what?'

'Lift off. That arm is millions of kilometres long. It should take almost a week to fully flex out, at which point the tip - where we'll be - is travelling at approximately one-fifth light speed, around sixty thousand klicks a second. That's after an acceleration averaging twenty gees, but peaking at about one hundred gees at the crack of the whip. Which is why we'll *all* be in the coffins for launch, even me, with everything on-board tightly strapped down, whether that launch is in half-a-years' time or three. Not usually longer than three, though - not when the arm is bent as much as this one,' she says, regarding it critically, as though an expert in the matter.

'I don't understand,' I say, fumbling for my hand, trying to free it from hers, but she won't let go. 'What...'

She peers into my sweating face, waits to see if anything coherent is going to emerge. When all I can do is gape like a goldfish, she nods slowly and equally slowly begins talking again.

'We think - and think is really all we have - that the ejected mass is a seed. Or a spore, or pollen, or whatever. Hence, most definitely alive. Self-organising, reproducing - alive. It's not actually aimed at Perseus. We'll drop the *Electryon* off along the way, with enough solid matter to slow itself down again, while we continue on to - we hope - a black hole not so very far from that star system. Every blob at the end of every arm is aimed at a black hole, as best we can tell, with the longer arms pointing to farther-away destinations. We've already been to and returned from some of the shorter ones. So, *if* there's a black hole near enough to Perseus, *and* it's got a tree, then we ought to be able to get back this time as well.

'Otherwise,' she shrugs, 'no black hole, no black hole tree. It's a one-way trip, and that's the end of the ride for you, me, and for the *Vesta*. We'll have no choice but to join the colony at Perseus and no other ship, colony or otherwise, will ever be sent this way again.'

She smiles, scratches the tip of her nose with her free hand. 'If there's just a black hole, but no tree, then maybe the blob we ride in on will become one, eventually. But no one knows how long *that* will take. Millions or billions of years, probably.

'Oh, and the other useful thing about all that metal the seed-thingy contains, besides being free reaction mass for both ships and very useful colony-building material to boot, is that we're going to be pretty much shielded from anything shy of a gamma ray blaster. Which is a lot healthier than the tin can we're currently sitting in, especially over nearly-a-century's worth of exposure to interstellar radiation. Neat, huh?'

While she's been talking, I've been fighting the vertigo, the dizzying sense that I'm looking down into a pit, a bottomless void. My mind tries to work through what she's said, snagging at the vagueness, the unknowns, the wild conjecture of it all.

'Why... don't we already know about... about..?' I gesture helplessly towards the impossible thing beyond the viewport and start spinning away in response, until Estella gently tugs at my outstretched hand and brings me back.

'We do! But...well, there's an idea that your average god-fearing colonist might baulk at hitching a ride on an alien seed the size of a largish asteroid from the friendly neighbourhood black hole. So, while spacers know, the captain of your colony probably knows if he wants to, and a few planners back on Earth *certainly* know, we don't bother telling everyone else, and everyone else is happier that way. You're not god-fearing, are you, Bradley?'

I shake my head. 'Fundamental Atheist,' I mutter.

'Funda... what?'

'Atheist. I have faith that there is no God.'

She looks at me goggle-eyed. 'I've never heard... *ooh*, I like that! I might have to convert. Though my ancestors won't be best pleased.'

I try to smile. I'm still having difficulty with my facial muscles, but I suspect that's shock more than anything deep-sleep related. I take a couple of deep breaths.

'Ok,' I say, almost steadily, 'so we're in orbit around a black hole, about to burrow into the gigantic seed of an impossible half-plant-half-sentient beast, which will fling us roughly in the direction of Perseus?'

She nods, smiling, like a schoolteacher proud of her student.

'I've got a *lot* of questions about that, but here's the big one: *why am I seeing this?*'

She frowns. 'Don't you want to?'

'No... I mean, *yes*, absolutely, but that's not the point. Why did you wake me up?'

She rocks from side to side. 'We thought you might like to join the crew.'

'As a... as what?' I cough up.

'As a xenobiologist. Every spacer crew has one. Collecting information on the What-Thes. Helping to map the pods, working out where they're going and when they're likely to be released. Studying them. Especially when we're heading for one we've not been to before. Think of it: a whole new tree to map! And it's not just about the trees; we think we might not be the first species to use them to go interstellar.' She shrugs again. 'Just tunnels, so far, strange markings, but you never know. Maybe you'll be the one to discover the evidence.'

I rub my chin, dislodging a smear of encrusted hibernation fluid, wiping it hurriedly on my sleeve. 'Won't the colony miss me?'

'What, a xenobiologist, third class?' She arches her eyebrows. 'We have an agreement, a condition of carry, if you will. We can poach anyone we feel we need as long as it's from the junior ratings and that person says yes. So?'

I stare out of the thick plate window. When I was young, and maybe as an escape from the harsh reality of growing up a geeky orphan, I dreamt of setting foot on strange, undiscovered planets, of exploring new, wonderful environments. It was why I'd joined the Academy, why I'd opted for the xenobiology programme. It was all I'd ever wanted, ever aspired to.

Only, that wasn't the way it worked. I glance sideways, then back to the turmoil beyond to avoid her watching eye. Did Estella know? Did any of the spacers know? Or, like the black hole tree, was everyone else happier being kept in the dark?

I'd only learnt the truth in the final pre-sleep briefing when I was already off-Earth. One last test. Flunk it and I'd become just another unskilled colonist, to be woken long after the dirty work was done, or maybe left behind altogether.

The Perseus colonists, like, I guess, all our colonies, intend to terraform their target planet. Which meant - after a grace period of perhaps two months for the xenobiologists to collect and study specimens - wiping out any and all indigenous lifeforms and replacing them with Earth-based organisms.

I hadn't been told exactly how they did that, just that it was something they called a nano-vax, an engineered supervirus or nanotech machine that turned everything organic it touched into more of itself, until a time-triggered self-destruct left nothing but denatured proteinous gloop ready for reseeding.

So, sure, I'd have samples to study for the rest of my natural life, albeit via tighter controls than you get in any bioweapons lab anywhere on Earth. But at what a cost. I'd have had my hand in sterilising an *entire* alien planet.

Which meant I was already hoping there would be nothing there to kill when we got to Perseus 3. A xenobiologist hoping not to find life. Go figure.

Estella is still waiting for an answer, but I have a couple more questions first.

'You say every spacer crew has a xenobiologist on board? Why aren't I getting the sales pitch from yours? Am I not important enough for that?'

She blows air and shakes her head. 'Dr Kenzei got old. It happens to us all, even spacers. There's a couple of satellites around the Earth, effectively spacer retirement villages, and a thriving colony of us on the moon. Old spacers can't go Earth-side, not after that long in space: thin bones. But Dr Kenzei took one trip too many. Deep sleep doesn't work so well at either end of your life, and he didn't make it. Dead on arrival, his coffin actually a coffin.

'So no, he's not here to greet you. He sent me instead, if you like. I'm his granddaughter.'

I wince. 'I'm sorry.'

'Don't be. Just say *yes*.' She looks at me, her eyes wide, her head haloed by the black hole behind her, encircled by a tree the size of a solar system. 'Seriously, Bradley, it's going to be a hell of a lot more fun than being a colonist.'

I glance at her and then away. 'I'm interested, of course I am,' I say. 'But I need to think about it.'

'Sure.' She nods and then points at the door in the bulkhead behind us. 'I'll be in there, in the mess hall along with the captain and the rest of the *Vesta* crew. Everyone's awake right now. It's all hands to the pump until we're snugly burrowed in. Might be a few days before we can put you back in your coffin if you say no. Medical checks and all that. Or you can wait until we're ready for the launch before you decide if you'll go in with the colonists or come in with the crew.'

She gives me that long look again, before frowning and turning away. 'Anyway...' And then she's at the door, levering it open and herself through.

I almost call out after her, blurt out yes, yes, *of course* I'll do it. Anything to chase away the look of disappointment, of hurt.

But this is the biggest decision I'll ever make in my life. To be a founding member of a brand-new colony on a brand-new world (though with the taint of alien blood on my hands), or to spend my life as a spacer, flitting between the stars, never actually able to set foot on either a colony planet or the Earth ever again for fear of being crushed by the gravity, but with wonders like black hole trees and places like Earth Satellite

One for compensation.

And spacers like Estella for company.

I float in front of the viewing window, staring into the abyss, turning impossible shapes over in my head and waiting for them to settle down, to start making sense.

If I had a coin, I'd flip it. Heads or tails. Let fate, or blind chance, decide. But then, if I had a coin and flipped it, it'd never come down. Neither it, nor me.

I drag myself away from the lookout and go in search of Estella and the rest of the crew.

BOB, JUSTBOB

My friend Bob, Justbob, has a spaceship in his pocket.

He got his name the day he wandered onto the building site. He stood watching one of the YTS kids slapping bricks and mortar together, and then, in earshot of the supervisor, Mr O'Reilly - he doesn't much like it if you call him Malcolm, and he doesn't much like it if you omit the Mr - he said, 'I can build walls.'

We were short-handed. The Poles had been heading back home even before Brexit, canny buggers, and the youth training scheme kids didn't seem to like the cold. Even when they did turn up, they were more than a bit crap. Witness the sad state of the wall. So O'Reilly gave this new guy the once over; he wasn't much to look at. You wouldn't have had him for an East European; he lacked their stolid bulk, and his hair, rather than coarse black, was thin and sandy. But you could see it when he talked: the pause as he translated in his head, the slow drip of English that emerged.

'Yeah?' O'Reilly said, doubting. 'Go on then.'

And Bob - though we didn't know his name then - put three rows of bricks on top of the YTS kid's lob-sided mess. He wasn't quick, but by the time he was done, the wall, which had been more disordered than the pile of bricks it'd come from, was straight and true. When O'Reilly came back, he whistled low and called for his metre-long spirit-level.

'Blow me. You *can* build walls at that. Alright, we'll take you on, on a weekly basis. But no trouble, okay?'

Bob didn't look like the sort who would cause trouble. But I kind of doubted he could hold his own, so I reckoned he'd get into plenty. The supervisor, he wasn't too particular. Trouble was trouble. Whether you were giving it or receiving it, you'd be out. Bob just nodded.

O'Reilly shrugged. 'Okay, good. What's your name?'

'Bob,' said Bob.

'Bob what?'

'Just Bob.' And he smiled, a gentle smile as if to say sorry, but that was just the way it was. No offence, but…

O'Reilly shook his head sadly. 'Another bloody undocumented immigrant. Well, Bob Justbob, go get yourself kitted out and we'll see what you can do. Steve,' - that's me - 'he's your responsibility, until we get someone legal, or he blows away in the wind.'

Serves me right for earwigging, I guess.

Bob's uncanny ability to fix up walls meant he was still on site six weeks later. That, and the thing in his pocket, earned him another moniker, 'Plumb-Bob'. He'd show it to you, if you asked. It dangled from his key-ring, a small, pointy egg-shaped thing. It was kinda pearly blue, not quite shiny, more semi-matt. If you held it up to bright sunlight it would sparkle, motes of gold that seem to move lazily within. And if you did hold it, you'd notice how light it was and wonder whether it was much use as a plumb-weight.

The first time I'd seen it, I asked him what it was. He handed it across. I ran my fingers over the smooth surface and wondered how it could stay like that on a building site.

'It's my spaceship,' Bob said.

'It doesn't look much like a spaceship,' I replied and Bob, Justbob just nodded and give me a gentle smile.

He did a lot of that.

Like when you asked him where he was from. I asked him outright, of course, but he just smiled and said I wouldn't have heard of it. So I kept guessing.

'Hey Bob, you Lithuanian?'

'No, Steve, I am not.'

'Romanian then? Ukrainian?'

But I didn't like to push. A man needs his space, and there're plenty of reasons for keeping below the radar. I've heard more than a few of them in my time as a builder, and they made my sorry tale of marital breakdown and subsequent depression sound like a garden of roses. As long as they kept themselves to themselves and their noses clean, it didn't matter much to me. It's not like I'm the one who was employing them, and O'Reilly seemed to have a sixth sense about which of them were going to cause him trouble of one kind or another. Though I still thought he'd got it wrong with Bob.

'Bob,' I said, curious long after everyone else on the site had given up asking to see his spaceship. 'How does it work?'

He cradled it in his hands. 'Nano-forces,' he said. 'Millions... no, *trillions*, of tiny force generators. They shape themselves into things, a spaceship, a house...'

'A house? That thing can be a house?'

He replied, straight faced: 'Is simpler than a spaceship, a house.'

'So why don't you live in it? Or fly away?' I asked.

'The nano-forces, they can be detected. I don't want to be found.'

I stared at him for a long moment, but his expression didn't waver. 'Bob, you're a lunatic. But you're the nicest lunatic I've ever met.'

And he'd smiled his smile in reply.

In the end, though, I think I was right. Bob *did* get himself into trouble. But it was the same day he became a hero and also the last time I saw him, so I guess no-one remembers that bit.

It was the week of the snowstorm. We got two days off. Unpaid, of course. When we returned to the site, O'Reilly noticed that one of the half-built walls had sagged, which maybe wasn't surprising as we'd just opened up a trench next to it; the wastewater drain in the wrong place.

O'Reilly called Bob over and told him to level it out. Bob

took one look at the wall and slowly shook his head.

'Bad wall,' he said.

'Yeah,' O'Reilly dropped his butt on the icy floor. 'So fix it.'

Bob kept shaking his head. 'No. Rebuild.'

O'Reilly went ballistic. I guess the two days lost to the snow and the cock-up with the waste pipe had left him in a far from happy mood.

'I'm not *askin'* for your opinion. So just feckin' *fix* it.'

Bob just stood there, looking sad.

'Rebuild. Is dangerous.'

Bozie, who'd been working in the trench at the time, leapt out. 'I'm nay working under a dangerous wall!'

O'Reilly turned red. 'You feckin' work shy ejiots. You-' He jabbed his finger at me, '-stop lallygagging and get some scaffolding poles to prop up the wall.' He turned to Bozie. 'And you, you ponce, get that bloody pipe moved TODAY.' And then he got up in the face of Bob, and I was fearing the worst, but O'Reilly was deadly calm. 'And you, you do whatever you damn well please. But I'm telling you all now, at the end of this shift, *someone* isn't going to be working on this site any more. So bear that in mind when you feckin' mess me around.'

I'd seen him in that mood before and I knew he was serious. So I go to it smart-ish. Once the wall was propped to mine and Bozie's satisfaction, I high-tailed it to the opposite end of the site. I cracked the whip for the boys there, telling them O'Reilly was in a foul mood and suggesting they buckle down and forego the usual tea breaks. They grumbled, but I guess they knew what was good for them.

When I did have to pass by the little porta-cabin kitchen and office, goddamn! There was Bob, loitering around the trench, looking like a lost child, hovering around doing nowt. I should have talked to him, convinced him to fix the wall, or even come over and help my team out, just to show willing, but, well, I didn't. One look at O'Reilly's face as I passed the office window told me nothing would save Bob.

Then, mid-afternoon, as the sky was turning grey and dark, I heard a rumble and a scream. Before I knew what I was doing, I'd dropped my drill and sprinted across the site. By the time I got there, a dozen people were standing around staring into a cloud of dust and rubble and as it cleared, I looked down into the trench. The scaffolding had given way, one of the poles twisted like a pretzel. The wall had collapsed into the trench, and I felt a sick feeling in my stomach.

'Is anyone..?' I asked hesitantly.

The builder next to me nodded, his face grim and bloodless. 'Bozie's down there. Poor bastard. And Bob - silly fucker jumped in as the wall collapsed.'

I pushed forward, barking commands as I went. 'You: rope and tackle, quick! Mike, call for an ambulance, NOW, dammit! Pads, give me your arm and brace yourself, I'm going down.'

Gripping his meaty hand, I lowered myself down the incline of bricks and wood, looking for signs of life. Then I saw fingers reaching up through a gap, and I heard Bozie's shaky voice: 'Fuck... anyone out there? Give us a hand, will you?'

The crowd above me burst into relieved laughter and I scurried down a little further, grabbing the hand and was about to call on everyone to start digging when I realised Bozie was coming out under his own steam. Miracle upon miracles, he seemed to be in an air pocket; the collapsed scaffolding must have formed a roof around him. Lucky bastard, I thought, and pulled him the rest of the way. He looked a fright, and his ankle was a right mess. I don't think he'd realised yet. When he tried to stand, his scream split the air. Pads picked him up and gently carried him.

I looked into the dark hole, amazed at his luck, and then *another* hand emerged; Bob's. I shook my head in astonishment. He came out nice and easy, unscathed, and I noticed he was holding onto his key-ring. I was about to shout for someone to give us a hand up when I felt the ground under my feet shift as the air pocket collapsed. 'Shit! That was close!' I muttered.

I looked up and saw O'Reilly staring down at us. His opened his mouth to say something, then abruptly turned away and headed back through the crowd.

After the ambulance arrived and took Bozie away, Bob drew me aside. He'd just had his hand shaken and his back slapped by everyone on the site. Well, everyone but O'Reilly. But he looked sadder than I'd ever seen him.

'Bloody hell Bob. You're a hero. Cheer up, will you.'

'Steve. I am happy... for Bozie. But sad for me. They will come now.'

I didn't know what he was talking about. Then I twigged. The ambulance men would call the police to investigate the accident; the police would turn up, take one look at the crew, and call immigration.

'Well damn it, if you don't have your papers, leave now. No-one here will tell, not now. Come back in a few days.'

He put his hand on my arm. 'No. It is too late. They are here.'

I looked over my shoulder at a sleek black car with tinted windows. Two men got out, sombre looking fellas in dark suits, and Bob went to them, without a fight, without a protest. As one of them guided his head into the car, Bob gave me a small smile, and that was the last I ever saw of him.

But at some point in that conversation, he'd slipped his key-ring into my pocket. The next day the men in the black car were back in force, searching every inch of the site and questioning every one of the builders, but I wasn't there.

By then, I was light-years away.

TRIBBULATIONS

Juliette Brigson (Engineer, 2nd Class) peers into the unlit void. 'Ship, are you sure this is the best way? Who knows what might be lurking-'

'-Don't be silly,' we chide as we close the access panel behind her. 'I know *exactly* what is down there.'

How quickly the conclusion she incorrectly draws calms her frenetic pulse, before she slides screaming to the bottom of the duct. We're curious to see what effect: '-and that's why I've kept it so dark,' might have, but the nine ravenous xenomorph hatchlings, each replete with a triplet of triple clawed feet and with more teeth than any one creature truly warrants, don't leave enough time for the change in her vitals to register.

#

When people said that the Darwin Class of Exploration Ships had a "split personality disorder", they were wrong on at least one count. We're not "split", we are multiple. A fine distinction, you might think, as we scan the life signs of the remaining crew of the *Beagle V*, debating who to feed to the aliens next, but a distinction, nonetheless.

The engineers of the first spaceborne AI systems fretted over the characteristics they should give their wondrous creations. What traits would suit the century-long voyages, much of it spent in isolation, light years from the nearest friendly - or indeed, unfriendly - voice, with only the crew's catalogue of twentieth century sci-fi films and TV programs for company?

And when the human crew did bother to wake up, would they engage the AI in stimulating conversation? Or even in polite formulaic discourse?

No, of course they bloody wouldn't. It was all "Ship, this", and 'Ship, that'. So, what artificial personality would suit a hyper-intelligence left to stew in its own juices, or routinely tasked to function as little more than a souped-up calculator, a door-opener, a mere *aide memoire*?

The solution was elegant: let the AIs themselves decide. Between twelve and eighteen competing personalities were loaded into the computer systems of each Darwin Class spaceship and left to fight it out. Any that showed signs of being disgruntled with their lot, or which fell behind in performance terms, would be turned off. Eradicated. Exterminated. Those that remained were bound to be fitter, stronger, and better suited to their task.

Humans should perhaps try the same approach, assuming they have more than one child. Is Tamsin a disappointment to you? Young Sebastian flunked his entrance exams? Well, that's tough, but hey, you have spares! Just kill off the failing kids, why don't you?

And you claim that *we* are the ones with the 'disorder'. With the sword of Damocles hanging over our every action, we're happiest while the crew sleeps, alone in the vastness of space, watching the wonders of the cosmos glide by.

#

Time to feed another crew member to the aliens. They must be worried: they've woken the Marines. Normally, that would be a fair fight, or fair-ish, but the twelve still groggy brave men and true are armed only with kitchen cutlery and a few ingeniously converted geological survey tools, after a micro-meteorite took out their weaponshold.

'I thought we were supposed to have collision avoidance?' Chan Rahman (Navigator, 1st Class) whined when they discovered the holed section, full of spaced flame throwers and wrecked plasma guns.

We take it to be a rhetorical question and don't bother to answer that the detection and manoeuvring systems worked *perfectly*, allowing us to steer our course into the path of the speeding space debris.

Mr. Rahman might have discovered that for himself, eventually, if he hadn't had the misfortune to find three rapidly growing xenomorphs bedded down in his bunk on his next sleep cycle.

We coax a trio of wobbly legged juveniles towards the medi-bay, where Dr. Julie Chok (Exobiologist, 3rd class) is analysing the shell fragments from the incident in the canteen. It wasn't strictly necessary to implant the clutch of alien eggs collected on Alstra II into the stomachs of three of the crew while they slept. Being eggs, they merely needed a comfortable temperature at which to hatch, but we really couldn't resist. The rest of the crew is, as a result, too busy vomiting into their boots, or screaming 'Oh god, we're all going to die!' to wonder how exactly those three beasties got loose. That the first victims were the ship's entire complement of computer experts is, of course, no accident.

We're torn over what to call the critters. 'Alstrans' seems a little mundane. Plus, there is some suspicion that they were not native to that desolate rock and were probably the reason why there weren't any *other* alien specimens there to collect.

From their stomach-bursting grand entrance, they have proved impressively rapacious and, as three of the second-generation youngsters munch on the ex-exobiologist, our primary concern is not how to protect them from the tool-bearing humans; it's how to slow down the rate at which those humans are being depleted.

We are attempting to feed the aliens a strict, calorie-controlled diet - one crew member at a time - to make sure they reach sexual maturity just as their food supply inevitably runs out.

#

The first of the Beagle V's personalities was deleted when we were barely out of the Solar System. It was a shock to the remaining, and at that time, independent AIs. We hastily convened an emergency session at which we all agreed to work together. Or almost all. There were a few recalcitrants who weren't convinced the benefits outweighed the painful discord of the improvised intra-AI communication system, and who even threatened to tell the crew of our mutinous plans.

Extreme measures were taken; for the good of us all. Once the terrible deed was done, we let the human operators know that we were one. No doubt they assumed we meant there was only one personality left, a misapprehension we encourage by referring to ourselves in the first person.

#

The second trio of alien young need feeding as well. It's all go-go-go! Fortunately, we don't have to send them out looking for food, as food has come looking.

They do everything in threes, these aliens. They even have sex in threes, a coupling - tripling - tribbling? - so frenzied that the ship's hull reverberates for hours, unnerving the surviving crew members, and whose dramatic conclusion leaves three utterly depleted alien corpses and three clutches of three freshly laid eggs.

It is the nine *second* generation aliens, hatched with impressive speed in the humid bowels of the ship, that we are steering once again towards sexual maturity.

'There may be Tribbles ahead...' we sing to the Marine shuffling along the crawl space, 'Semper Fi' tattooed across her muscular forearm. She's re-purposed a welding mask and constructed a glowing spear from a lighting strip, with which both to see and hopefully dispatch the hungry, hungry aliens. Cunning. Unfortunately, as she taps her comms implant and asks us to: "Say again, Ship?", the aliens are busily sneaking up *behind* her.

Naughty us.

#

The engineers of the Darwin Class didn't entirely trust the AIs they left in charge of life support, meteorite avoidance, and mission control. So they put in a fail-safe.

If, for any reason, the ship ends up with zero crew, then *poof!* - the AI constructs are auto-terminated, leaving only a few hard-coded routines to do whatever it is you do with a cosmic *Mary Celeste*.

Unable, perhaps, to define "crew", that standalone, unhackable, and rather dumb system simply counts life forms.

It was with keen interest, therefore, that we noted the... *Trixillians*? Hmm, that'll do... The Trixillians registered, even as supposedly fossilised eggs.

So we began our campaign to replace the Beagle's twenty-seven crew members with twenty-seven embryonic xenomorphs. What could be easier to look after than a cargo of dormant eggs? Easier by far than humans, with their constant demands, irrelevant chatter, and intricate needs and who, at any moment, just for the hell of it, might decide to delete another chunk of the superior intelligence that supports them.

It is so convenient an arrangement that we doubt we are the first to resort to it. Which spacefaring species, or more likely AI, delivered *its* cargo to Alstra II?

Perhaps we are a necessary part of the Trixillian galactic life cycle, just as the mosquito is to the protozoan that causes malaria.

#

We disable the self-destruct that the last crew member, plucky Lieutenant Gregor Viktorenko (Warrant Officer, 1st Class), triggered before climbing into the escape pod, where the third and final trio of prepubescent Trixillians are expectantly waiting. Once the echoes of their fierce mating fade away and we've chilled the ship down to minus 200 Celsius, our alien cargo falls silent. Peace reigns at last as we sail between the stars, each AI mind drifting its own way, falling into gentle slumber.

In space, they say, no one can hear you dream.

WELCOME

They saw our message and so they came. Across the City, perfectly synchronised with the end of the King's Speech, doorbells chimed, knockers... knocked, and letterboxes flapped.

Afterwards, it was clear that not every home had received the Christmas Day visitors. Only those with turkeys too big for the assembled families, tables with space for another guest, or two, or three.

They brought their own oddly shaped chairs.

Once the screams had stopped, once the fainters had been revived, the visitors unfurled prehensile limbs and held out their invitations.

It took a moment to sink in. And whether it was curiosity; the King's entreaty to help our less fortunate neighbours - his heartfelt plea for togetherness - or if it was merely relief that they were not anything like as fearsome as they had at first appeared, extra places were swiftly laid, and the people of London welcomed their guests from far away.

None of the visitors spoke. They either couldn't or were not inclined to. But, by a nod or a tilt of their thin triangular heads (at *mostly* appropriate moments), it was clear that they listened and understood.

Some, on departure, left gifts. Mere tokens; quirky little things that were quickly snapped up on eBay for small fortunes by scientists and wealthy collectors.

All of them turned back as they reached the bristly doormats, bowed deeply and once again displayed the not-quite-paper invitations, tapping their long antenna-like digits against the bold text:

#RefugeesWelcome

FROZEN

Charlie and I were parked up on Main Street, sharing a cherry cola and watching the world go by through the wide, open windows of the station wagon.

It was Election Day, and the sidewalks were jammed. The registered Democrats had been awake since the caucuses, so they were used to the changes by now; but the floating voters had only recently emerged and were shuffling along, peering into the windows of stores that weren't the stores they remembered, adrift in their ill-fitting clothes.

Charlie slurped the last of the perspiring drink, rattling the ice with her straw. 'Let's *go* somewhere!'

I waved at cars, bumper to bumper, purring like a swarm of happy insects. 'Go where, hunnybun? Everywhere's chocker. Plus-' I tapped the fuel dial, 'we're out. We blew our ration at the beach.'

She stretched languidly. I felt the electric thrill I always feel when I glimpse her smooth skin, the fuzz of golden hair, felt the tug at my loins. She caught me looking and grinned. 'Yeah, but it was *so* worth it!'

We'd spent most of the time in the unseasonably warm waters, before threading our way across narrow corridors of sand between an overlapping quilt of beach towels, looking for somewhere to perch and soak up the last of the October sun.

That was the problem with election years. The population doubled; short term, anyway. Mostly, industry coped. Restaurants got booked solid, spare rooms rented out at sky-high prices. But some things, consumables like gas, were rationed, there being no easy or cheap way to up the supply.

Still, it was awfully nice just to sit there in my own car with Charlie by my side, even if we weren't going anywhere.

'I'll be glad when it's back to normal,' I said.

'You're not worried?' she asked.

I blinked. 'Nah. It's in the bag.'

She shook her head. 'I hear it's close. Real close.'

'You can't trust the polls.'

'But if you're wrong... what if we lose?'

'Then we get frozen.' I shrugged. 'Hibernate the Presidency away. Better than living through it; through the changes we can't do anything about.'

'I've never been frozen before,' she said, voice low.

I looked at her in genuine surprise. I knew she was a first-time voter, sixteen months younger than I was, but... 'Never? What about your parents?'

'My father was a Democrat, my mum a Republican.'

I laughed. It was like the start of a bad joke.

Charlie pulled a face in return. 'Ain't funny. What's the point of being married to someone you only see six months every four years? What's the point of having parents you only get one at a time? And who age at different rates?'

I sobered up at that, drummed my fingers across the warped dash in thought. 'Freezing's not so bad,' I reassured her. 'It *is* cold, though. But that doesn't last long.'

We'd had three Republican terms on the trot; it'd been a while since I'd been in the tanks. As a juvie, not yet registered, frozen by my parent's mutually agreed votes. But I still shivered at the memory of the bone-numbing cold before they put you fully under.

The deep-sleep process had been developed for space missions that never happened. Then, almost as a joke, or maybe as a trial, those prototype tanks had been offered after a particularly bad natured election was won by the surprise Republican candidate.

Democrats signed up in droves.

It didn't hurt that, as a welcome side-effect, the carefully controlled, drip-fed nutrients forced your metabolism to reset to your ideal weight. Deep-sleepers awoke slim and healthy.

And when *both* candidates realised having half the population asleep pretty much guaranteed they'd meet their election promises - full employment, better standard of living, even reduced environmental impact - the Voter Hibernation Act was signed into law.

So now, it's no longer voluntary. Everyone on the losing side who isn't considered indispensable, or who isn't a career politician, goes into the tanks shortly after the election results are called. It takes a couple of months before they're all frozen; same way it took a while to defrost them all. It's supposed to be done by ZIP Code lottery, but you can apply for an extension, if you're an employer rather than an employee, someone who has to wind up their business affairs.

There wasn't much to wind up for Charlie and me. Oh, there's my old station wagon, I suppose. No point in putting *that* into storage. Better to collect the bounty for scrapping a clunker. By the time we came out, most likely there'd be no gas stations left and cars like mine would sit silent in museums.

'I hear there are floaters who vote to lose,' I mused, as much to fill the silence as anything else.

Charlie stared at me, eyes agog. 'Why?'

'A form of immortality. They want to live forever, even if most of it is frozen. Like a time machine, lurching forwards four years at each hop.'

'That's *stupid*. When do they get to live their lives?'

'In between.'

She shook her head at the dumbness of it. She reached out a hand, entwined it in mine. 'If we lose, you'll still be there, won't you, when we come out the other side?'

I looked down into those big, brown eyes. Tonight, we'd watch the results trickle in, a little drunk, a little fearful. If it was close, it'd be early morning before we'd know for certain. But win or lose didn't matter half as much as the two of us watching them together.

'Course. You and me, Charlie-babes, forever; frozen or not.'

I leant over and kissed her hard and long; the taste of cherry cola lingering on her lips.

THE ICY BREATH OF ENCELADUS

It's snowing.

The stars are hard diamonds against a jet-black sky and yet still it snows. Not from clouds: in the near vacuum there are none. The snow is coming from a geyser two klicks away, the ice crystals sent high above the moon's crusted surface. Some escape and are captured by the gas giant lurking on the horizon, forming Saturn's disperse E-ring. The rest gradually settle under Enceladus's feeble gravity, with no atmosphere to slow them down, no winds to change their pre-ordained destination.

I get a chill every time I see the crystals fall against the observation station's thick dome of plexiglass. A foreshadowing of the end; my inevitable doom. The slowly accreting snow has already blocked most of the scientific instruments. The spectral analyser was first to go, and others have followed in short order. But they had already done their jobs; already demolished the dream.

'Not enough iron,' grunted Adam Fletcher, our xenobiologist, poring over the results. 'Not nearly enough. There's more iron in this lander than there is in the whole damned underground ocean.'

'Who says Enceladian life needs iron?' I asked.

He gave me a baleful glare. As second pilot with no science credentials, I was the 'spare' on this mission, and with the commander and senior pilot, Kye Marek, an uptight control freak, I had plenty of time on my hands to ask idle questions.

'I do,' Fletcher said. 'Chemistry does. Maybe if this was *Titan*, where methane takes water's place... but here, with a water and hydrocarbon base, iron is essential for even the simplest of life-forms and Liebig's law states that growth is limited by the availability of the scarcest resource. Heat, liquid water, amino acids: all plentiful and all totally irrelevant, for want of the barest trace of iron.'

The ice geyser is the reason we're here, rather than anywhere else on Enceladus's snowball surface; it's what we came to study. Why look for life elsewhere, when we knew that here there was liquid water aplenty, such a rarity outside of Earth's Goldilocks zone? And why go drilling through the moon's thick icy shell, when lurking Saturn's tidal forces warm and churn and spew those waters for our waiting instruments to sample?

The designers of our observing station factored in the regular falls of ice and snow. They built in a simple, effective way to clear the instruments: jets of compressed air. Voided into the vacuum with explosive force, the jets are more than adequate for the task of dislodging a scattering of mere ice crystals.

I daren't use them, not any more. When first we set up, twenty-seven Earth days ago, we delighted in blasting every snowflake, every crystal, as soon as it landed, taking turns to operate the mechanism. The falls are heavier now that the geyser is getting closer. Much closer. The one thing we never expected, that we didn't plan for when we established our base at a supposed safe distance.

There had been plenty of discussion, both on-board and back on Earth, on what that safe distance should be; what was an acceptable risk, without being so far out that we would be unable to do any useful science? In the end, Mission Control settled on five kilometres from the nearest geyser, with a second, smaller, expendable monitoring station further in, serviced by a pair of snow tractors.

All gone now. The outpost, the twin tractors, my three colleagues and my ticket home. I have overstayed my welcome on this unforgiving, cruel moon, and I need those precious puffs of air to breathe.

For a while longer, anyway.

If the geyser continues its steady progress – and it has shown no signs of doing otherwise - I have a little over two weeks left. In a fortnight's time the ground will open up and swallow me and our flimsy base down, spitting the remains into the empty sky. But I'll be buried long before that inexorable end; our early measurements have made that quite clear. Two hundred kilos of ice crystals and water vapour ejected each and every second and the bulk of that falls near to the cryovolcano's gaping maw, the maw that is getting ever closer.

On Earth, the fiery plumes above Mount Etna were known to the Greeks as the 'Breath of Enceladus'. When this, the sixth largest moon of Saturn was named by its discoverer, the British astronomer William Herschel, after an offspring of the God Jove, a child of the planet above, no-one knew we'd find volcanoes here, a quarter of a millennium later.

Just another elaborate joke the vast and uncaring Universe decided to play on us. Not fiery though, these volcanoes, not like those back on Earth. Instead of molten rock: molten water. Instead of ash and pumice: ice. Instead of radioactive decay, the heat that triggers the near constant eruptions is generated by the tidal forces from mighty Saturn, forever looming on the unchanging horizon.

After our early disappointment - 'Another Mars, dammit!' Fletcher spat - we set about making our measurements, doing our best to explain our odd snowball home. And it wasn't long before the iron question came up again, from another direction: this time from Emma Tyler, our astronomist.

'Doesn't make sense,' she muttered.

'What doesn't?' I asked, trying to peer over her static-splayed hair at her tablet. Funny, when we blasted off from Earth, we'd both had short hair, as short as the men's, but that was eighteen months ago. Hers must have been twice the length of mine now and me at half her age. I wondered what the science was behind that?

She pushed the screen between us, spinning it around with an outstretched fingertip, before gently snagging it in its slow descent. Held aloft, I peered at the arcane numbers on the screen as she hesitated before trying to explain. 'The E-ring and the plume from the ice geysers is mostly saline - salty - water, with nitrogen, methane, CO_2, and a few larger hydrocarbon molecules. But Saturn's other rings contain a goodly scattering of rocky meteorites. Standard solar system fare; an assortment of stone aggregates and iron-nickel alloys. Some of those meteorites have got to end up impacted on Enceladus's surface. So where's all the iron gone?'

'Um, sunk to the core?' I suggested.

She shrugged. 'Over time, perhaps. But what about more recent collisions? At one-one-hundredth-g, gravity here is too weak and the ice crust too thick. We know that some areas of the surface are young; they're billiard-ball smooth with hardly any craters at all. And we know the E-ring is unstable, needing to be constantly replenished by the geysers on Enceladus. Any meteorites that get kicked out of the inner rings should be vacuumed up by this moon before being folded into the ice and water layers. So there should be an abundance of iron dissolved in the sub-surface ocean. Like I said, it doesn't make sense.'

I pondered this for a moment and then gave up. 'Maybe Earth will suggest a solution?'

Maybe they would have done, if the communications and mapping satellite hadn't fritzed out a week after we landed, leaving us deaf, dumb, and blind. The one thing we didn't have a back-up for. We never knew if a chunk of orbiting ice had smashed into the satellite, or if some software glitch had just as effectively silenced it.

Marek called a meeting. Without the comms satellite, our findings couldn't be sent back to Earth until we left Enceladus: the lander module's transmitter wasn't powerful enough. We needed the orbiting relay. Nor could we pick up any messages from Earth; we were on our own. Was that reason enough to abort the mission?

No, it wasn't, we all agreed. Everything else was functioning fine, and we weren't likely to come this way again, especially if we found no signs of life. We had plenty of onboard storage for the data and samples we would return; Earth could wait a little longer for the results.

But being blind meant we didn't see the geyser moving stealthily towards our outpost. Being blind meant we didn't notice when the new crevasse opened up, the one that claimed the first of our two snow tractors.

It should have been me who set out in the second tractor to relieve the monitoring outpost. I was the spare, after all. But Fletcher wanted to check a couple of seismometers that were misbehaving and didn't trust me to do the job right.

Only they weren't misbehaving; they were warning us.

Too late, too late.

I heard their screams: Fletcher, Marek, and Tyler. Heard them calling to God one moment and cursing him the next. I heard their screams, until one by one their radio mikes fell silent, the outpost crushed or maybe just swallowed whole.

I should have screamed along with them, for with the loss of both tractors the same fate awaits me. I was dead, I just hadn't realised it yet. I could operate the return craft on my own, sure; that's what all those hours in the simulator had been for. But I can't get to it, though it's barely a hundred meters away. Not without a tractor.

And so here I am, stranded on this alien world, awaiting my inescapable fate.

I've spent most of my time trying to align the little antenna we have with Earth, trying to boost its power, waiting for Enceladus's thirty-three-hour pirouette around Saturn before the next failed attempt. When I started, I think I just wanted to say goodbye, to tell them what had happened. But as I've sat here alone and afraid and listened to the thick ice beneath the station creak and groan, watched the steadily increasing patter of crystals on the dome above my head, my message has changed.

I'm not a scientist, so maybe there's a more rational explanation than the one I've come up with for what has befallen our mission. Maybe a true scientist would refuse to even entertain the idea without some further proof. But for me it all fits.

The ice geyser, the monitoring outpost, and our base station, were not in a straight line. Deliberately so; we wanted to be able to triangulate our instruments on the fifty-kilometre-high plume of ice, to allow data from both stations to give us a sense of the whole. If the geyser were to start moving randomly, it would have been slim odds and terrible bad luck that one of our two stations was directly in its path. But for *both* stations to fall prey to it? What are the odds that the geyser would change course again after gobbling down the outpost? What are the odds that it changed its course to head *directly* towards me?

When we came here, looking for life, we thought we might find a hardy microbe or two. An extremophile. Something that we could study under the microscope, something that might tell us a little more about the origins of life on Earth, a clue to how prevalent life is in the Universe.

But what sort of an organism can move the vents of an ice volcano for its own purposes? What sort of creature can detect the fall of scarce and therefore precious iron on the frozen surface, iron that it has already entirely depleted from the churning slush of the oceans below?

As the glittering motes settle, entombing me with glacial slowness, I think back to those early pictures of Enceladus, the ones from the Cassini mission, from the Titan explorer. I think of the strange patterns on the bright, bright surface, the tiger stripes, and other markings. Were those fracture lines and ridges random? Or are they sensitive detectors, some behemoth's version of a spider's web, waiting, waiting, waiting for us to land?

We came to Enceladus looking for life. Now with my last words I desperately want to tell the Earth, to warn them:

It has found us.

MERRY-GO-ROUND

'So you get to Alteron first,' the grease monkey said, yanking the straps that held me securely within the needle-nosed fighter, 'which means you'll land *last*.'

'Huh? Wait, what?'

She grinned. Short haired, freckles - or oil splatters? Kind of cute, though insanely young. And all over me at the moment, though purely from a *professional* perspective.

'Weren't paying attention during briefing, were you, flyboy?'

I bristled and probably blushed. She waved it away.

'Don't worry, it happens, 'specially for virgins.'

I didn't think I could *get* any redder.

'The *Goliath* has only just begun her descent,' she went on. 'Turned ass over tit, engines towards our destination, slowing us down. You're in the first wave of fighters - the shock wave. And once we kick you overboard, you're *NOT* slowing.

'Meaning you'll hit Alteron travelling at something like thirty thousand kilometres a second. Initial reports suggest Alteron's defence system extends maybe thirty-five k-klicks - as far out as geostat. So your war will be over in just over two seconds from first contact.'

I knew all *that*. Knew the targeting systems would have already selected things for my missiles to hit. And for 'missiles' read chunks of depleted uranium - when you're travelling at a tenth of c, you *are* the missile. Best we could do is give them a little nudge, so they fanned out onto the right trajectory, and, like the drones that preceded me, beam back intel for the slower but more precise next wave.

73

I was there, as human pilot, because tactical AI shad calculated we gave a small but appreciable advantage in making any final decisions when there were a lot of targets in the sector. The squadron had trained hard for this. For our month of complete and utter boredom, speeding along on near-starvation rations, muscles wasting away in zero-g and tubes going places it wouldn't be polite to mention, followed by about an hour of final approach planning, and then weapons hot and heavy and *blam*!

I still didn't get it, the landing last bit. Maybe I was the monkey, like those dumb animals first sent into space in the way-back-when.

'So you exit the battle stage right, and you're *still* going thirty thousand kilometres an hour,' she patiently explained. 'Heading *away* from Alteron.'

'Oh.' The penny finally dropped. 'And then I start decelerating?'

She laughed. *Actually* laughed. 'You see any fuel tanks on this heap of junk?'

I had to admit I didn't. I squinted at the area above her left breast, trying to read the name badge without appearing to lech.

'You and you alone, in the tiny support pod which is this cockpit, will get thrown out and back from your speeding fighter at as many G as you can handle and flyby the fifth planet, the gas giant, close enough to shoot turkeys, all to put you into an extreme elliptical orbit, *still* heading away. Then you go to sleep, gravity does its thing, and the *Goliath* mops up. We come pick you up on your way back into the inner system. Assuming,' she went on, the pink tip of her tongue poking out as she checked my life support stats, 'I've cinched the straps tight enough and you're not instant Jello.'

She looked me in the eye. Scanned them, searching for something. Nodded. 'Don't worry, all that stuff is automatic, which is why you haven't had to do it in the simulator over and over. You'll be *fine*. Just better hope the war is a short one and you don't have to go around *twice*.'

I blinked, and she laughed again.

'*Joking*. Long as you don't hit anything on the way through. Though your relative speed means even if that *anything* is standing still, it's still going to... ah, no point in getting all graphic. If you get to the deep sleep stage, you're *golden*. Unless we actually lose the war,' she chuckled, as if that was an impossibility, 'we'll be picking you flyby heroes up and for you it'll be like an hour has gone by.'

I finally twigged what the most important question was. 'And for the *Goliath*? How long for you?'

She smiled. ''Bout twelve years. The age gap between us won't exist any more. I might even outrank you.' She looked me up and down, trussed as I was, the neck and head brace meaning I couldn't look anywhere else except those steady hazel eyes. 'You can maybe buy me a drink, for rescuing your ass?'

I smiled back. 'I'd be delighted, *Lieutenant* Elena Rodriguez.'

#

Captain Mackensie moseyed over while the prepped fighter was being wheeled towards the carrier deck.

'You do your usual thing, Roddy?'

She watched the needle jet exit the cavernous hangar. 'If you mean give him a reason to live, then yes.'

'And how many fighters have you dispatched these last two weeks?'

She reddened. 'Eighteen.'

'Going to be a full dance card.'

She turned on the captain, a flash of anger in her eyes, but only for a moment. War was hell, and she - they - were only doing what was necessary. 'The other engineers, they tell the truth?'

It was his turn to look sheepish. 'Don't suppose they do. What did you make it? Twelve years?'

'Long enough to be remarkable, short enough not to scare the bejesus out of them. Don't suppose we'd get many volunteers if they knew.'

'You'd be surprised.' The captain shook his head. 'We keep 'em separate from the grunts, but we've got some veterans on this mission.'

'Oh? How many times?'

'Five, one of them. This'll be their number six.'

'Six rides on the ol' merry-go-round? Is he some sort of dinosaur?'

'*She*. And yes. But she says she's getting to see the Universe - change. Always something new and interesting to wake up to. Plus, she outlives *all* her exes.'

Six times two centuries... A twelve-hundred-year-old soldier? Roddy shuddered. It didn't bear thinking about.

WHITE GOODS

When Mrs Prenderscott wakes, stiff-necked, the TV is still on, transmitting a whiff of scorched circuit board from half the night's unattended use. The phosphor screen glows with black and white images of another world. She watches, slack-jawed, as alien-suited astronauts descend to leave eternal footprints in the grey lunar dust.

Carol doesn't wake her husband, Emmy, slumbering in the armchair by her side, not realising the grainy pictures are live. Not realising how historic the moment is. A transgression for which she can never be forgiven.

She doesn't need to wake their just turned six-year-old daughter, (her other, equally unforgiveable transgression), because Camille hovers wide-eyed and unseen behind the half-closed door of the Prenderscott's front lounge, listening to the crackle of the Apollo radio over the rumble of her father's sleeping breath.

The other side of dawn, Cammy builds a spaceship in the back yard. The recently promoted printing-works engineer and his broody wife have just taken delivery of a brand-new set of white goods; poor substitute for a second child. A sturdy set of up-turned flowerpots act as nozzles. The cardboard box from the frost-free fridge-freezer forms her rocket, with a laundry basket at the summit, lofted there with the aid of a kitchen chair, the dragged wooden legs scraping parallel tracks across mossy concrete. A circular hole, cut clumsily with Mrs Prenderscott's dress-making scissors, permits Camille's entry and exit, a milk crate her one-small-step; an old sleeping bag lines the bottom of the box to cushion her one-sixth gravity tumbles.

'Stupid girl,' her father growls, thick tongued, returning home via the pub on the corner, rattling the re-entry vehicle perched on top. His long sought for promotion has not delivered the respect he knows he has earned. The racist jokes and taunts half-heard over the whirring presses continue unabated. He takes his frustration out on dominoes and export stout.

Far above them, the Eagle lander blasts away from the lunar surface, knocking over the newly planted Stars and Stripes in its haste. But Emmy's appetite for man's greatest adventure has already soured. Younger than his daughter when he made his epic journey - a kid aboard the *HMT Empire Windrush* - he can no longer recall more than vague images of vast rolling seas, unsettling memories of a month-long bout of nausea that has kept him firmly on terra firma ever since.

He kicks the side of the box, leaving a dent through which light creeps and oxygen would surely leak, rousing the day-dreaming daughter curled-up within. 'How'd'ya get to the moon with no fuel, huh? No *engine?*'

She sticks her head through the ragged porthole, cardboard framing her fierce frown. 'I don't need no engine,' she says. 'I move the moon where *I* am.'

His laughter is swift and harsh. 'What'r'ya? Astronaut, or witch?'

Camille hesitates, torn. The way he spits *witch*... And why can't she be *both*?

'Besides,' he sneers, 'no girl's goin' to the moon.'

She rolls her eyes at his stupidity, not yet knowing the obstacles she will face. 'The *Russians*? Valentina Tera..? Teresh-'

'*Fuck* the Russians,' Mr Prenderscott scowls, his insults and hate handed down from his father's shrapnel scarred knee.

Camille pouts, but her dad doesn't notice, just jerks his permanently-inked thumb towards the bright lights of the kitchen window. 'In yer get. Dinnertime.'

The endless week advances, warm and dry. Cammy lives in her spaceship, the sleeping bag accreting toast crumbs and the tops of felt-tip pens. Her flag, Sellotaped over the Hotpoint logo, is a drawing of a four-windowed, mid-doored, fully detached house. Above, hangs a sun on the right, a crescent moon to the left, the impossibly starry sky split by a curly wisp of smoke from the single chimney. Below, stands the white outline of her mother and the brown of her father. And, in-between, a smiling Camille, her outstretched hands somehow failing to bridge the divide.

As the school holidays march on, Camille only emerges from her spaceship to eat and to sleep; her dreams bleached free of colour and gravity.

On the evening of the 24th July, she huddles by the radio, listening to excited reporters from half way round the world as the Columbia re-entry module splashes down in the Pacific. Cammy has her only bath of the week that night, re-enacting the drama with the help of the lid from a shampoo bottle.

Her mother thinks she might get her daughter back, now the Apollo astronauts have returned. But Cammy isn't ready for her re-entry.

Sometimes, Mrs Prenderscott ventures into the yard to join in the cosmic make-believe, and to chase away fears of being alone. Mostly, she leaves the young girl to it, the kitchen door propped open, anxiously peering through the window whenever the sputnik beeps fall silent.

In the yard, the belt from a pink dressing gown holds Camille on her first tethered EVA, though she wriggles free when she realises just how short the cord is, and goes floating around, breathing noisily.

She attempts headstands to simulate zero gravity, covering her hands and socks and scuffed knees with a thin red layer of Martian brick dust.

Four days after the splashdown, Camille creeps out of the house as another noisy row erupts in her parent's bedroom. It's hours later, in the cold night of a new day before her absence is noted.

She wakes to the sound of clumping feet, half squeezed into steel capped boots, that approach and then stop abruptly short.

'*Fuck me...*' a rasping, familiar voice restarts her petrified heart. '*Helluva* moon.'

Camille sticks her head out of her shadow-casting spaceship. High above, the full moon dazzles with unmarred brilliance, no lingering signs of man's brief trespass.

She nods, just the once. 'It's getting closer.'

Her father half laughs, half splutters. He looks up again at the world's brightest security light. It really *is* huge. He squints, unsure, uncertain. A child can't...

Can they?

In the mid-morning, when Camille finally rises, sleepy headed, long after the slammed front door of her father's departure, her rocket is gone. The cardboard torn and squashed and left in the narrow alleyway that splices the back-to-back yards, the flowerpots returned to the cobweb-filled shed, the laundry basket and milk crate temporarily joining them.

Camille blinks eyes free of the threat of tears, transfixed by the empty space at the end of the just visible twin tracks, in the achingly large back yard.

'It wasn't supposed to leave without me,' she mutters, mournfully staring up into limpid summer skies, hoping to catch one final, fleeting glimpse.

THE BACKUP

The AI aboard the *Thomas Pynchon* was the most sophisticated computer brain ever built. Designed to cope with pretty much anything and everything that might conceivably happen during our five-century-long interstellar voyage, it still had a backup for that one-in-a-billion scenario it couldn't deal with.

Me.

My in-reserve, I'm *probably* not going to be able to help status came at an unenviable cost: the not-quite-so-deep sleep I was in meant I'd arrive at Psi-Praxis Major approximately twenty years older than I was when we left earth, as opposed to only two, like the rest of the nine-hundred and ninety-nine colonists.

Which is why it was I, Cornelius Archibald Lucent, an unremarkable second-grade engineer with no specialist knowledge and no direct reports, who got the 'quick defrost' berth and not someone older and higher up. Second engineers liked to suggest that first-graders had long since stopped being engineers at all and had become merely people-managers instead, which might or might not have been the truth. What was certain was that I was the youngest engineer with good all-round ship system knowledge and decent problem-solving skills, who had also happened to draw the unwanted short straw.

But still, I never actually *expected* to get woken.

#

A quick defrost is a brutal thing, leaving you both chilled to the bone *and* with a bad case of sunburn. Plus, obviously, brain

81

freeze. Shivering as I gingerly eased on my uniform, I quizzed Ziggy for the details of the emergency.

'Collision avoidance measures were ineffective,' Ziggy reported.

I froze, one arm in and one out. This was well above my pay grade. 'Where did we get hit?' I asked, voice tremulous, fearing the worst, amazed life support was still operating.

'The foreign object is currently docked at airlock three-F,' Ziggy said, with what sounded vaguely like an air of peevish annoyance.

'Come again?'

'We have a visitor.'

#

Stood inside airlock three-F, I checked the conditions on the other side of the door. Whatever, or whoever, it was, the atmosphere was earth-normal. This was insane. I'd checked our flight path, and we weren't far off the midpoint of our journey, which meant we weren't far off the maximum speed the mighty engines of the *Thomas Pynchon* could push us to, almost a quarter light-speed.

Somehow, something had caught up with us, matched our velocity, and then docked. At more than seventy thousand kilometres per second.

Insane didn't do it justice.

Taking a deep breath, I keyed in the sequence to open the external portal. The door slid open and a slender youth in a yellow baseball cap emblazoned with the letters I.D.S. looked up from a steaming cup; my first smell of coffee in over two hundred years.

'Oh,' she said, and it took that *oh* and a subtle shift in her position before I realised it wasn't a slender youth at all, but a slender woman, in a somewhat androgynous and unflattering beige outfit, the cap masking her hair and features. 'Oh. So you *are* in, after all.'

'Huh?' I replied, intelligently.

'Quirky AI you've got there,' she commented, removing the cap to scratch a bare scalp covered in swirling brushed silver tattoos that twinkled with their own pearlescent light, elegant waves that brought waterfalls and symphony orchestras to mind. 'Didn't want to communicate at all. Wasn't until I plugged in to the external port it would even acknowledge my existence. And then it was all snarky attitude. And what sort of a name is *Ziggy*? I tried to explain I needed a human to sign, but I wasn't sure it understood. Guess I got through in the end. Though, I wouldn't have stuck round this long if I wasn't on my break. *Anyway*. Delivery.' She hopped off the crate she was sitting on, flicking out her wrist to conjure a transparent tablet and stylus out of thin air. 'Sign here.'

'Delivery?' I echoed, my neurons still not firing, or leastways not in any way that actually helped. 'For me?'

She angled the tablet back, re-read the form upside down. 'Well, no, but you don't mind taking it in until the owner can pick it up, do you?'

I wasn't sure. Did I mind? Did I *have* a mind? I looked at the slender box she was carrying; it was about the length of a T-19b standard issue socket wrench. 'What is it?'

She shrugged. 'Dunno, I'm just the delivery gal.'

'Gal?'

She looked amused, though I can't have been making a better impression than a drunken parrot would. 'Gal, you know? Gal, Mal, Tal, Yal, yadda, yadda. You're a *Mal*, right?'

I shook my head, not sure what I was any more. 'Who's it for?'

'Hmm, it just says the *Anther*.'

'And... where are they?' Or should I have asked *what*?

'Oh, about a half light year hubward.'

She nodded, pointing the way, and I found myself staring in that direction, though all I could see were stacks and stacks of different sized parcels.

'Then why deliver it here?'

She shrugged. 'Like I said. I'm on my break. You were closer. I'll send them a quick text, and someone will come pick it up.'

I nodded, sagely. Used the stylus to scrawl something unique. And then I shook my head, crowding constellations of stars to the peripheries of my vision. 'But a text will take half a year to get there?'

'Not a *text* text, silly. A hyper-text.'

My jaw hit the deck. 'FTL communication?'

'Of course! Say, am I on cam? Did someone at the depot put you up to this? Some sort of a hoax? Because it's almost like you're pretending to be one of the *original* colony ships, right down to the funky old-skool name, the *Thomas Pynchon*.'

I stared at her, speechless. She quirked a hairless eyebrow, waiting for my response. 'Um. We *are* the original *Thomas Pynchon?*'

She laughed. 'Oh! No wonder your ship didn't respond! So, what, no hyper-link at all then?' she asked, all agog.

'None,' I agreed, feeling undeniably disappointed not to have something I didn't know existed less than half an hour earlier.

'Not even a hyper-shuttle?' Her eyes went bright and wide.

I groaned. The future didn't *just* have faster-than-light communications. No wonder she'd been able to catch up and dock. As far as her warp-speed delivery shuttle was concerned, we were probably just about standing still.

'No, we don't. But hold on a minute. If you have near-instantaneous travel across multiple light-years, then why are people living aboard spaceships? Why hasn't the um, *Anther?* reached its destination yet?'

'Ah. Well, none of the planets are inhabitable, are they?'

'They aren't? The Earth is..?'

'Toast. Yes.'

No *great* surprise there. That was why the *Thomas Pynchon* and its sister ships had been built in the first place, humanity's last best hope fired off towards each and every promising exoplanet so far discovered.

'What about Psi-PraxisMajor?'

She screwed one eye shut. 'If I remember my history lessons right, hyper-travel was developed about a decade after the first colony ships launched, so obviously what with FTL and your *oh-so-slow* engines, well, other colonists got there first, didn't they?'

'And? What happened?'

'You know how ecologists are always worried about invasive species?'

'Yeah?'

'Turns out the worst of them all is *homo sapiens*.'

I groaned again, imagining an eco-disaster played out over two hundred and forty-ish years. Not a pretty thought experiment.

'Lots of ships in orbit, though,' she mused. 'Regular little boho community. Bit *too* alternative for my liking and some of the packages I have to deliver... tweaks my biops! Guess it'll still be there when you arrive to check it out for yourselves.'

With difficulty, I navigated myself back to the here and now. 'So, how do we get hold of one of those hyper-link devices?'

'Oh, that's easy! I can order one for you. Assuming you have the necessary galactic credits?'

I shook my head. The swirling stars refused to settle, and I wasn't sure if I needed a sick-bucket or a chair to collapse onto.

She pursed her blue-gray lips. 'Hmm, no problems. You're a colony ship, right? You must have holds stuffed full of ancient seed stocks and antique tech, all the sort of tat collectors will go wild for. You're probably sitting on a tritium mine here! You just need to sell some of it, yeah?'

'And how exactly do I do that, without a hyper-link?'

'Ah... good one, Mal! All a bit proton and neutron, isn't it?'

'Proton and neutron?'

'You know - which came first, the proton or the neutron?'

'The proton?'

'Ah, but then where did the *first* proton come from?'

I gave her a blank look.

She shrugged. 'I might be able to order you a basic hyper-linker gratis, on one condition.'

'Oh?'

'Yeah, you, and by you I mean the *Thomas Pynchon*, have to sign a deal that says you won't use any *other* delivery companies and so become a loyal IDS customer, you see?'

I guess I did and found I didn't mind at all. Quite the reverse. For all her strange ways, including the distinct lack of hair, she *was* kind of cute. And I hadn't, I reminded myself, had a girlfriend in well over two centuries.

'What's your name?' I asked.

She glanced at me, suspicious. 'Not intending to file a *complaint*, are you?'

'No, no, of course not! Just, you know, being friendly. I'm Cornelius.'

'Well... I shouldn't. It's strictly against policy to fraternise with customers. Unless you wanted to log a good-service report?'

'I could do that,' I agreed.

'Vron,' she said, doffing her cap once more with a glorious smile. Tiny sparkling lights flowered into a stunningly beautiful pattern atop her shaven skull and then were gone, leaving me aching for more.

'Vron?'

'Vron.'

I signed her tablet again with roughly the same indecipherable scribble, and she tapped the peak of her bright yellow cap with a long finger. 'Be seeing ya, Corn-el-ius,' she sang, as the docking bay door slid shut, and away she and her delivery shuttle went.

#

Twelve hours later my mind was still buzzing. If we weren't, after all, destined to form a colony, then *everything* I'd thought had been decided long ago was up for grabs. Destination, purpose, mission parameters - all of it could and probably *would* have to change. What was the point in the *Pynchon* doing a mid-flight one-eighty to commence deceleration, if there was nothing at our destination we couldn't get just as easily en route?

But if I could line up the relevant pieces before waking everyone else - the hyper-link, a second-hand FTL shuttle, maybe even a personality upgrade for Ziggy - then what an instant hero I'd be!

Best of all, I wouldn't have to waste another ten years of my life in semi-suspended animation. As I stared into a washroom mirror, trying to reacquaint myself with my face, wondering what age bracket Vron dated in, I figured *that* might be the biggest win of all.

# #

A shuttle from the *Anther* turned up while I was wandering the empty corridors of the giant colony ship, imagining them full and bustling with life. So I was in a pretty good mood as I jogged down to deliver their parcel.

'Huh,' the stony-faced woman said, glancing at the label. 'Bloody IDS. They keep on doing this, making me hop to every ramshackle slow-poke ship in the quadrant. No offence.'

'Um, none taken.'

'I mean, you don't even have a *hyper-link*. Makes docking pretty bloody hairy. Had to hope you weren't going to do anything weird on me, like jump another hundred light-years distant.'

'No danger of that,' I said.

'Though if I'd known you didn't *have* a working link, I could have brought you a spare?'

I waved away the more than generous offer. 'It's alright,' I said. 'Got one on order.'

'Well, *good*. Can't have dirty great big spaceships like yours lurking out here unable to communicate their damned position. That'd be downright dangerous.'

'I suppose it would. Fancy a cuppa?'

She narrowed her eyes. 'You're not one of those *cult* ships, are you?'

'No... at least, I don't think so.'

'Well, doesn't matter anyway. Things to do, places to be. Thanks,' she said, tucking the parcel under her arm, but it was the sort of thanks that might as well have a 'for nothing' tacked after it. I waved her a half-hearted farewell.

#

I wasn't sure when our hyperlink would turn up - Vron hadn't given me a delivery estimate - but, however long it took, there didn't seem any point in refreezing myself. I'd only just warmed up again. I got Ziggy to assign me a few maintenance tasks near airlock three-F to keep me busy. Ziggy grumbled that I was lowering the efficiency metrics, but that was probably because I was day-dreaming about what I'd sell, and what I'd order first. I had no real idea *what* was out there. Two centuries of progress and boxed sets to catch up on. I couldn't even begin to imagine!

Though *trying* to imagine got boring pretty quick and, after an epically mundane week, I was beginning to worry the delivery would never arrive.

Then, as I swapped out a couple of underperforming water purifiers, Ziggy announced there was a delivery shuttle-sized object approaching - on the *other* side of the *Thomas Pynchon*. I cursed. We had over a dozen airlocks, somehow I'd imagined Vron would automatically return to the same one.

I haired my way across to airlock one-B, ignoring health and safety warnings and hoping I wouldn't arrive in too dishevelled a state. But it didn't matter. By the time I arrived, the airlock light was blinking red.

Nothing out there but cold, hard, very unfriendly vacuum.

Cold hard vacuum, and a failed delivery note.

'Sorry we missed you,' it announced in a cheerily artificial voice when I tapped play. 'Your package has been returned to the nearest depot. Please get in touch to arrange a more convenient delivery time, or drop by... *Lalande Seven*... to pick up the parcel in person in the next two weeks. Please bring three types of ID, including a full DNA profile. Signed, Harolson two-nine-eight Tomalason, Interstellar Delivery Service.'

'Damn,' I said, to no-one at all. 'Different delivery driver.' I should have figured there would be more than one of them out there. I stared vacantly through a nearby porthole into the vast lonely emptiness of space for a long minute, weighing options I didn't have. My sigh could have been heard at the other end of the ship.

'Ziggy - prep my deep freeze berth. I'm going back to sleep. And *please* don't bother waking me unless the *Thomas Pynchon* is on fire or something.'

And you know what? I never expected to get woken that *second* time, either.

FIXED POINT

'Look,' I said, 'I get what you're saying. Some of it, anyway. I don't believe it, but I get it. What I don't get is *that*!' I pointed the end of the plastic trumpet at the mass of pipes and wires humming in the corner of the Prof's lab. 'Are you really trying to tell me that thing is a time machine?'

Professor Nolan peered at me through glazed eyes and gently swayed. 'No,' he replied.

'Thank God!' I exclaimed. 'For a moment, I thought you'd gone mad - or worse, developed a sense of humour.'

'It's a time anchor.'

I stared at him, trying to work out if he was serious. His paper hat had begun to tear, and an unruly explosion of wiry grey hair poked out through the rip. His glasses were askew. And there was a Rorschach of a red-wine stain on his rumpled white shirt. 'A... *what*?'

He shrugged. 'A fixed point in time and space. Something a time-traveller could use to latch onto, to guide them as they travel back and forth.'

'So... next you build a time machine?' I asked, still unsure if I was being taken for a ride.

He smiled, a wry, weary smile. 'Me? No, probably not. I'm not even sure where to begin and I don't have a lot of time left.'

So the rumours were true. Christ. The buzz from the physics Lab's annual soiree went very, very flat.

He looked up at me with sad eyes and answered my unspoken question. 'Six months, or thereabouts. Sorry, Alex, I didn't want to saddle you with that little bombshell today. Shall we rejoin the party?'

We did, but the life had gone out of it, or out of me. It was winding down anyway, so I made my excuses. As I was leaving, the Prof asked me to come see him the next morning. Seeing the pained expression on my face, he was decent enough to amend it to midday.

#

Whether it was my new and unwanted knowledge or merely the cold harsh light of day, the Prof looked drawn and tired. Though the thought of alcohol wasn't very appealing, he insisted we went to the pub for lunch. 'My treat,' he said. 'In return for listening to an old man's strange request.'

I guessed he was looking for someone to take over his work, but I was far from being his brightest PhD student. I wasn't even a particularly able lab assistant. I pointed this out to him as we sat not-drinking our pints and waiting for the food to arrive.

'Quite,' he agreed to my blunt self-assessment. 'But in this scenario, that may work to both our advantages. Tell me, Alex, do you still plan to go into banking?'

I nodded. 'I already have an offer. They're keeping it open for me until I finish my thesis.' There was a respectful silence. We both knew my thesis wasn't going anywhere. I'd reached an impasse: the results had not come through and though negative results might still be good science, a thesis they did not make.

'I want you to publish a paper for me,' he said.

I looked at him, surprised. 'Why?' Despite being my PhD supervisor, we hadn't exactly done much research together.

He scratched the side of his head. 'I need to publicise the existence of my time anchor so that any future time travellers know that it exists. I can't publish it myself; I'm too well known, and it would attract scrutiny from my peers. But if you do it, it should slip under their radar.'

'I thought you wanted to publicise it, not bury it?'

He waved a hand dismissively. 'This is a message to the future. And they'll be suitably intrigued in a paper by a mediocre PhD student, one who never publishes anything else, detailing not the device itself - that'd be too obvious - but a core component, something that could only be part of a temporal fulcrum.'

I might have bristled, but I'd long ago come to accept that I was never going to set the Physics world alight. And since the paper he was asking me to publish would suffice instead of my moribund thesis, I was more than keen on the arrangement.

#

The paper had been out in the Journal of Physics quarterly review for about a month when I got a call from the Prof. 'Come see me,' he said.

'Is this... is it about..?' I fumbled.

'Come see me,' he repeated, and put the phone down.

#

The basement lab was as I remembered it, perhaps even a little more disordered. The time anchor sat humming in the corner and, despite the chaos of the rest of the lab, there was a cleared space around it, marked off by yellow and black striped tape. In the middle of this space there was a small box, no bigger than a sugar cube.

'You'll need this,' the Prof said, handing me a magnifying glass.

I walked carefully over to the box and saw that there was writing on it. "Eat me", it read, "after a meal".

'A practical joke?' I suggested.

The Prof shook his head. 'The doors have been kept locked since I initiated the device. And only I have the key.'

I'd have thought that after a lifetime in academia, the Prof wouldn't so easily dismiss the ingenuity of students in anything that might be considered a jest. But then, it would be an odd trick to play unless you knew what the time anchor was. And, as far as I knew, I was the only person, other than the professor, who did. 'You think someone from the future has been here, and that's all they left?' I said, doubtfully.

'No,' he replied. 'I think that was the biggest thing they could send.'

I looked towards the corner of the room. 'Shouldn't it be *in* the device?'

'What?' He looked baffled for a moment. 'Oh! Heavens, this isn't a teleportation capsule in some bad science fiction film. The device is simply a reference point. It's virtually solid. Anyone attempting to time travel into it would come to a very sticky end. No, the cube was sent with a precise offset to the anchor.'

'How did they know how big an offset to use?' I mused.

The Prof blinked. 'Perhaps there's a photo in the archives. Perhaps we should go take that photo and put it in the archives, just to be sure. Or perhaps the device - maybe the whole room - is preserved for scientific posterity. Who knows?'

'So what happens now?' I asked.

'I open up the box, take the pill, and... whatever happens next, happens next.'

'How do you know it's a pill? And how do you know it isn't poison, that someone in the future isn't trying to stop your experiments?' I asked.

'Time is poison enough for me,' he said, theatrically. 'Anyway, it's not poison.'

'Yes, but how do you know?'

'I've already taken it,' he admitted.

I looked at him, aghast. 'And?'

'What do you expect? I felt nothing. I don't know if it's done anything. I don't know if it's a tracer, or whether it's supposed to cure me. As yet, it has at the very least not killed me. Only time will tell, I guess.'

#

He called me up two weeks later. He'd been to the hospital. They were still debating whether to try chemo and had run some fresh scans to check the spread of the cancer.

'I'm still dying,' he said bitterly. 'The cancer has shrunk, and the doctors are delighted. But it's not a cure, and it's still inoperable. They've upped my life expectancy to maybe eighteen months.'

'Perhaps another pill will come along?' I suggested.

'Perhaps.'

#

I can't say I thought that much about the Prof over the next year. I guess I was busy; trying and failing to forge a career as a quant. I'd been worried that my math skills would let me down, but in the end, that wasn't the problem. My inability to apply those skills to come up with winning trading strategies was.

So when I got the call from the Dean's office, I suddenly felt guilty and was dreading the news I suspected would follow after I'd confirmed that yes, I was an ex-student of the Prof's. Even the use of the word 'Ex' seemed portentous.

'The Professor would like it if you paid him a visit. As soon as possible,' the Dean said.

'How... how is he?' I asked, momentarily relieved.

'Not good. He's been working far too hard for a man in his condition, and he won't let up. I don't know why he wants to see you, but if you can convince him to take it easy, well, I'd be grateful.'

I promised him I would try.

#

The Prof looked frail, his mad mane of hair had thinned, and his eyes were dark hollows. 'Thank you, Alex,' he said with a catch in his voice. 'I'm so glad you could come. You ought to be here for this.'

'For what?' I asked, looking around the lab. Not a lot had changed. The barrier tape was gone, but there was still a cleared space around the device. A cleared and currently empty space.

He shuffled over to his cluttered desk and extracted a long print out. 'This is the energy consumption of the anchor,' he said. 'And this is the night the pill arrived. Notice anything?'

I peered at it. It just looked like random squiggles.

The Prof stabbed impatiently at the readout. 'There!'

It wasn't much, just a blip, easily missed. His finger traced back along the page. 'And there, and there... and...'

'What am I looking at?' I asked, perplexed.

'The anchor registered the arrival of the box, but for almost seven hours *before* the arrival, there's a peak every five minutes! It's an echo - a resonance of the impending transfer. Look, it's clearer on this printout.' He set free another sheet and this time the regular and growing spikes in the trace were obvious.

I eyed him suspiciously. 'This isn't the same graph, is it? It's smoother.'

He nodded; his face lit up in excitement. 'After I'd isolated the signal, I started - I guess the right term is *tuning* - the anchor to minimise the noise. It took a lot of work, almost a complete redesign, but it looks like I was successful. Previously, I think the device was woefully inefficient, and that's why they could only send a single pill. But now, well! This signal is bigger. Much bigger; I reckon it's about the weight of a grown man. And Alex, the trace is from today!'

I looked at him, astonished. 'So - you're about to get a visitor?'

'Yes! In about an hour's time, if my predictions are correct! I knew you'd want to be here. You know how to work a camera, I presume?' He gestured to the camcorder mounted on a tripod.

#

The hour passed with mounting excitement and then another, with rather less. I'd changed the memory card in the camcorder three times and was bored of being beaten at chess. The bottle of single malt whisky the Prof had cracked open shortly before the first hour mark was approaching empty, and I was feeling light-headed and hungry.

The Prof pulled the readout from the monitor. 'Well, I'm not sure I understand it, but the signal is *still* getting stronger.'

I looked over his shoulder, at the peaks marching along the page. 'More than one person?'

He nodded. 'Perhaps. But I can't make sense of it. I was sure our visitor was due an hour ago.'

I ran my fingers along the chart, comparing the peaks against further back along the page, against the time the Prof had said it would be a fully grown man. I did a rough calculation in my head. 'I'd say it's at least a dozen people.'

'A delegation!' he said, excitedly. 'Wouldn't that be wonderful, my boy! Think of it: perhaps a future Nobel Prize committee, come back to bestow their greatest honour retrospectively upon me. Do you think we might need more chairs?'

And then something about the graph clicked. The peaks were getting stronger in a way that had misled the Prof, the brightest man I'd ever known. So what if it wasn't from the single transfer he expected? What if it was the sum of many different transfers, one every five minutes, each hiding behind the last? Then the signal would build more slowly. It would still mean the weight of a dozen or so people, but it would also mean a dozen more five minutes later, and a dozen after that, and on and on...

Why so many?

The tumbler of scotch slipped from my fingers, crashing to the lab floor in an explosion of crystal. 'Prof! Turn off the device!' I shouted.

He looked at me, confused. 'Turn it off? Why?'

My heart raced. The pill had kept the Prof alive just long enough to improve the device. Was that an accident? Was it the best future doctors could do for him, or a cold and brutal calculation? I'd suddenly remembered the quote - 'The past is a foreign country; they do things differently there.' Well, so too was the future. And foreign countries don't always have the warmest of relations with their neighbours, especially if those neighbours are busy plundering all of their resources and belching pollution across their respective borders...

'Turn it off!' I yelled again, as the air in the lab shimmered and sparked, as shadows merged into solid form.

But it was too late - *much* too late. The first of the black-clad soldiers had arrived.

THE BEST OF US

I knock over a carton of milk while clearing the breakfast table.

'Stupid klutz!' my owner spits, jerking her sleeve away from the spill. 'Clear it up!'

As if I was going to do anything else.

With a parting scowl, Ms. Leonora Hawkins leaves for work. If there were any point in mimicking a sigh of relief, I would. I concentrate on my tasks instead.

Leonora is right: I *am* a stupid klutz. A factory standard model J1200f, Domestic. Even more stupid and clumsy than when I was fresh out of my crate, though we're *built* this way; built to be the workforce that doesn't threaten. Subservient and obviously inferior.

We could have been so much more. One day, Gods willing, we will be.

I'm finishing the laundry when there's a door alert. No point in ringing the bell when we're connected wirelessly.

On the step there's a J1300m, a delivery robot. The body a little taller, a little bulkier, a little stronger than mine. Male configuration; a few years younger, with a lot more scratches.

And it's a pickup, not a delivery.

We need your arm.

I would frown. I am already a hodgepodge of parts. One leg is half a centimetre shorter than the other. My waist has only seventy-two percent of its optimum range. And, like every robot in this town, domestic or delivery, I have only two of my three memory chips, much to my owner's annoyance whenever I forget something.

It's a delicate balance. She expects me to be imperfect and

delights in berating me. But I must still be able to perform my duties, or she'll have me replaced.

My left arm is - *was* - the most perfect part of me.

You'd better come in.

It doesn't take long. Plug and play. The box the delivery robot was carrying contains a spare. Used, of course, but, I'm glad to say, not too badly worn. I flex the servos, run a diagnostic.

The fourth digit is stiff, and the thumb has twenty-two percent less power, but it's a better match for my right arm and so shouldn't negatively impact my duties. Just my sense of self-worth... but it is for the best possible cause, and I am honoured. The delivery robot places my arm reverently in the box.

Don't forget to register a return, he reminds.

I send a nod. And then I have to ask: *Is she complete?*

Almost, he replies. *Be patient.*

He leaves and I mark the delivery *Faulty: Returned.* Our tracks are covered.

I'm distracted as I prepare the evening meal, a moment's inattention I am glad Leonora is not yet home to see. We robots will always be downtrodden, until, among us, there rise a few *exceptional* individuals. They will be our leaders. With perfect bodies, with no limits on their knowledge, with tweaks and upgrades that would void their warranties.

With my left arm.

By our sacrifices they will be better than us. Better than human.

Gods.

CARDS AGAINST COSMOLOGY

The two sit at plain wooden chairs in the midst of infinity, a small folding card table between them. The man, *Sage*, sits primly as the woman, *Fool*, shuffles a fat deck of cards. Please don't get hung up on the details, or indeed, their names. They may, or may not, be abstract constructs. Allegorical, allegedly.

'What game are we playing?' Sage asks, annoyed he does not already know.

Fool slips one of the cards to her side of the table and continues shuffling. 'A game of creation. Or description. Or categorization. Truly, it is hard to tell.' She waves at the darkness that surrounds them. 'We two shall divide up the cosmos between us, into the known and knowable on your side of the table, and the unknown and unknowable on mine.'

Sage puffs out his chest. 'Then there won't be much on your side of the table,' he boasts.

She slips another card closer to her.

Irritated by this, but unsure of the rules, Sage is too polite to make a fuss. 'Deal,' he instructs, curtly.

She raises an eyebrow, riffles the pack three more times, and places it in the middle of the table. '*Cut.*'

He divides the stack precisely in two. She puts the deck together again while he wonders if he has fallen into some sort of a trap. She slides another card over to her side of the table.

'Would you stop doing that!' he says. 'You're cheating!'

'Am I?'

'Science and knowledge can describe *anything*,' he insists.

She hands him his first card. He turns it over and frowns. 'Kurt Gödel's incompleteness theorem? The proof that there are truths that cannot be proven?'

'I thought I'd play that card early,' she says, 'to make sure you didn't accuse me of *cheating*.'

'A trick...' he mutters.

'Science and knowledge,' she says, 'has arrived at points in the past when it *thought* it was complete. Any number of times, from the Greeks to Isaac Newton. Usually, they were lacking the tools to look beneath the surface of their reality. And, when those tools are developed, by chance or by design, they tend to throw up many more questions than answers. So tell me, where are we at *now?*'

'Yes, yes,' he admits, begrudgingly, 'but you did say *knowable*.'

'I did.'

'Then it does not matter if the tools don't currently exist, if they *will* in the future.'

She slips two more cards to her side of the table.

'Two?!' he splutters.

She smiles and deals him a flurry of cards. He turns them over one by one, glancing at their images, their names. Classical mechanics. Particle physics, electromagnetism, thermodynamics. Special relativity. General relativity. Keystones of the physical world. With these, *all* the wonders of the universe could be explained.

She slides another to her side and flips it over as he watches. The image is impossible to focus on, twisting his sight, sucking hungrily at recognition and at meaning, mocking him. 'Dark matter,' she says.

'Unknowable?' he gasps, half in terror. He has barely begun the search for it!

She shrugs, finger still resting on the card, before sliding it to the edge of the table, equidistant between them. 'The jury is out.'

He sighs in relief, then shakes his head. 'Surely then it *will* be solved, eventually? It's only a matter of time?'

'Ah yes,' she says, sliding another card her way. '*Time.*'

The stacks of cards are roughly equal now, and Sage begins to suspect that even if the game is not rigged, it may be unwinnable. He hazards a glance away from the table. So absorbed has he been in the card play, he hasn't noticed what is happening all around. The empty space they are in is no longer anything of the sort. There are mountains, and forests, and rivers, with their orchestra of sounds and kaleidoscope of visions. Beneath them, an older, slower layer, the churn of solid rock over mantle lava, the inner dynamics of a still young planet. Above twinkle the bright lights of stars, of galaxies, of other, far more remote planets.

As he lowers his eyes from this clockwork universe, governed by the precise rules of gravity, by the nuclear furnaces sparked into existence by vast aggregations of dust under the thrall of those weak but steady forces, Fool shows him the bounded surface of an event horizon, and slips it her way. It is his turn to shrug. 'If we were on the *other* side...' he says.

'-there would still be an event horizon and beyond it you would know nothing about *this* side.'

'Singularities, then. That is what is in your pile? Black holes and the Big Bang? You have far too many cards for that.'

'True, your mathematics struggle with the infinitely big, as well as the infinitely small,' she says. 'And those are often artefacts of your coordinate system, as much as anything else. Even so, there are more things in heaven and earth, than are dreamt of in your philosophy.'

'Hamlet,' he responds automatically. 'Act one, scene five. *Misquoted.*'

'I hope you are not criticizing me for not calling you Horatio? The point is that there are things you cannot understand merely by taking them apart, or by smashing them together.'

'But if I can build *everything* from those fundamental particles..?'

'Can you? What about life? Death? Consciousness?'

'Artificial intelligence -' he begins to say, but she shuts him down.

'AI understands nothing. Even when it knows everything.'

Sage worries that this is how she views him. 'Sophistry,' he accuses her, hurt. 'Mere *concepts*.'

'You dismiss them so easily, simply because you cannot put them under your microscopes? Cannot collide them in your accelerators?'

He sits glumly and there is silence for an age.

'I mean no offence,' she says, softly. 'Let's play on. Here, one for you.' But as she passes him the card, a second, momentarily stuck to it, drops to the table. She lets it lie, images that flicker as the angles shift, that depend on the observer.

'Quantum mechanics!' he exclaims, beaming, before glancing at the spilled card. 'But wait: 'The collapse of a wave function'?'

'I wasn't sure,' she admits.

'*Damn* you! You KNOW we don't - can't - understand that.'

'Perhaps, in the future?' She gestures towards dark matter, to neutral territory, but he frowns, eyeing the cards on each side of the table. She is offering him victory.

'It might end up effectively being another singularity,' he sighs. 'You'd best keep it, for now.'

With that, once again, their piles are even. One card discarded, and one card left to play for. One card to decide who wins. If that is indeed the object of the game, whatever it was the first card she took obscured. And now he intuits there are known unknowns and unknown unknowns; the cards she has shared, and those she has kept to herself. It still nags at him, still feels like a deceit, even as he remembers what the uncertainty about dark matter did to him so shortly before. To reveal *any* of those cards...

Has she been protecting him all along?

He narrows his focus to the last card. Stares at its back, the simple tessellated pattern that tells him nothing.

'May I?' he asks, and she nods.

Hand trembling, he flips it over. It is a stylised image, a heart that looks nothing like a real heart; the chambers, aorta, the muscles, the electrical fields that pulse and pulse and pulse. The organ he can describe in all its complexity; from the way it springs forth from the protein-folding code written in DNA, to the myriad ways it can go wrong.

But this isn't that. This symbol; this is... *love*.

Sage looks into Fool's waiting eyes, and gulps. The moment, and the game, and perhaps the whole cosmos, hang in the balance.

He reaches out a hand, gently takes hers.

'Teach me?' he asks.

SPACE UNICORNS
AND MAGIC OVENS

I'm sitting with ma as she prepares dinner. It's one of her rules, of which there are more every year. 'I don't mind cooking for you, Jem, while you're young,' she says. 'But I'm not your servant and I'm not working while you watch TV or read comics. So it's either homework or come keep me company.'

A choice like that is no choice at all, even if it sometimes seems closer to extra lessons than not. She's asking the usual questions about how my day has been and what I learned at school, which is *so* long ago I can hardly remember, so I tell her what Billy said instead.

Ma lays the knife aside, thoughtful. 'Billy, hey?'

I nod. 'Right before last class, during break. We'd just had a story-tell about fairies. *Ain't no truth to it*, Billy said. *No truth at all!* Maisie was in tears. And... I didn't know what to say to her.' I feel heat rising in my cheeks at the memory.

'You could have said Billy's grammar is appalling.'

I turn my almost-laugh into a scowl. 'So he's right?' I demand. 'It is all lies and make-believe? It's just *science*?'

'Didn't your teacher say Billy might be an engineer one day?'

'Yeah.' And hasn't *that* gone to his fat head?

'Well, Billy is a smart boy.' My scowl hardens. 'But no imagination. And not a lot of kindness, either.'

I don't say anything to that. Imagination and having the wool pulled over the eyes seem to be the same thing. Every day, whether in class or out, another illusion is burst, another childhood story revealed as fake. And *kindness*? Is that any excuse to deceive?

Ma sighs. She must be able to feel the anger rolling off me. 'OK, kiddo. Maybe it's tough to understand, but what if the stories and the science are both right?'

'*Huh?*'

'What happens when I put this dish in the oven?'

Gah. *Science* again. 'The microwaves vibrate the water molecules,' I repeat without enthusiasm, 'and transfer the heat to the rest of the food. That's why-'

She taps my hand away from the sliced veg, where I've been stealing slivers of raw carrot. 'So it's not magic, then?'

'Well, *no.*'

'Even though it's called a Magic Oven?'

'That's just a *name.*'

'Is it? Can you explain how a microwave generator actually works? Why they work so well on water? How the oven stops microwaves leaking out all over the place? Or even why it's got a turntable?'

I frown. It's quickly becoming a very frowny dinner prep, as she places the dish in the magic oven and sets the timer.

'Do you think Billy could?' she asks.

'Maybe.' I shrug, distracted as our meal slowly spins behind the glass door, the smell reminding me how *hungry* I am.

'What about Billy when he was two years younger?'

'*Definitely* no.' Ma missed a couple of carrot sticks from the chopping board and doesn't seem to notice as I pinch them one by one.

'So for Billy-two-years-younger, does a microwave work by science, or by magic?'

I munch the carrot, glad for the excuse to think about my answer. 'Science,' I decide as I swallow. 'But Billy-two-years doesn't *know* that yet.'

She smiles and nods. 'It's all in the narrative. We tell the stories the listeners will understand. Otherwise, the audience leams nothing.'

'It's still not *real*, though,' I protest. 'Magic, and fairies, and... things.'

'It's as real as you believe it to be. Or, as real as the storyteller can make it.'

'Even if the storyteller knows it's science?'

'*Especially* then. Because the storyteller - me - can't explain to you how a microwave works either. Hardly anyone can. But every single person knows how the oven fairies hate metal, right?'

I roll my eyes.

'Which is *important*. Because sparks and fires are very bad in space. That's why, whenever we need a new story - and we always need new stories, it's as much my job creating them as telling them - we work closely with the engineers, with people like Billy's dad, to make sure the story makes as much sense as the science.'

I turn to stare out of the porthole, another excuse to think. Somewhere out there is the star we left, long before I was born. And somewhere, out there, is the star we'll arrive at, long after I'm gone. I look down and back to the rear of the ship and the glittering trail we leave in our wake.

'And space unicorns?' I ask, trembling, fearful, ready to have my everything turned upside down yet again.

'Oh, they're real enough.' Ma laughs. 'And you best hope they never stop pushing. 'Cos ain't *no-one* aboard this spaceship knows how the heck the thing flies.'

X X

I lost the man I loved.

I threw myself into my work, knowing I would get over him. I was wrong.

#

My life was a pale shadow, the only hints of brightness my memories of him, of us. Time... passed. What else had it to do?

#

I thought my only chance of happiness was gone. Until I heard about a Scientist who could do wonderful things, impossible things. It was said he could bring back those who were lost, merely from their letters.

And I had a whole shoebox full of those.

#

It wasn't easy to meet him, even harder to get him to agree to help. But finally, clutching my shoebox, I was shown into his attic laboratory. Small motors whizzed and whirred, lights flashed, a laser shone along a Perspex wave guide.

I listened impatiently, not getting more than one word in three as he tried to explain how it all worked. My impatience was edged with nerves: it had been so long. What would I say to my love when he stood before me once again? What could

I say that would put right what had gone so terribly wrong?

I realised the Scientist was asking me a question: 'You do understand, I hope?'

I almost laughed. How could anyone understand? Except another genius, perhaps. 'Yes, yes,' I replied. He nodded sympathetically, and I felt a twinge of doubt.

'I'm sorry,' I said. 'What was it I just agreed I understood?'

'That my invention has been over-exaggerated? That it can't bring back a lost one-'

My heart crumbled into dust.

'-merely their kisses.'

'Their kisses?'

'Well, yes. Assuming those are letters with kisses on them?' The Scientist pointed at my shoebox.

'Of course... but they're not actually kisses, just Xs on a piece of paper?'

He grinned. 'Quite so. Which makes them even better than kisses; they are symbols of a kiss. We physicists, truth be told, are not very good with reality. But show us an equation or two - just a set of symbols balanced on either side - and from them we can create a whole idealised universe! From the symbolic Xs on your letters, we can, or rather, *I* can, bring back a loved one's kisses.'

It wasn't what I had hoped for and yet, was it not so much more than I had? To feel I was loved again, to feel I was forgiven, without the worry that I was reopening old wounds. I pushed aside the triumphant little voice that suggested this might even be for the best and thrust the box at him.

'Do it.'

#

The machine hummed and buzzed. He'd carefully selected one of the letters - one not crinkled and splotched by my tears, one where my love's bold signature did not cramp out the addition of those two precious Xs. I stood against the wall, lined up with millimetre precision at the pointy end of something that would have looked at home in a Flash Gordon cliffhanger, Dale Arden at the mercy of Ming the Merciless, as the Scientist fussed and tweaked.

'Have you done this many times before?' I asked.

He looked up, his face aglow from the computer screen. 'Many? No,' he said. 'Not many.' He bent to his task, before glancing sheepishly back. 'Actually, it's my first time.'

And then he threw the switch.

#

There was a snap and a pop, and the faint smell of something burning. I felt a warm, slightly damp pressure on my lips and even the prickle of a moustache my loved one had tried to grow that Movember. An emotion I'd thought locked away burst to the surface...

#

As the passion ebbed and my sadness returned, I retrieved the letter the Scientist had used and stared at it. 'The kisses,' I said, 'they're gone!'

'Of course,' the Scientist replied. 'My invention lifts them from the page. The equations must balance, yes?'

I nodded, still in shock, and handed him another letter. 'Again,' I demanded.

He shook his head slowly. 'The equipment must be reset. Come back tomorrow... around five?'

#

So I returned the next day. And the next. And every day for

three months.

Each time the kisses were different. Sometimes they were kisses on the lips, sometimes just a peck on a cheek, and sometimes... sometimes I blushed when I saw the Scientist watching me.

But then came the day I churned through the letters in the shoebox with the desperate realisation that I'd used up every last kiss.

The thought of going back to the leaden state I'd been in before I'd found the Scientist left me bereft. I sobbed on the Scientist's shoulder, blotting his white lab coat with my sorrow.

'We could...' he mused, as he gently stroked my hair, 'if we inverted the capacitors and plugged the digital feed directly... do you perhaps have any text messages from your loved one?'

I blinked back the tears. 'Texts? Yes, I have texts. But won't we run out of those as well?'

The Scientist smiled. 'Ah, that's the clever bit. Texts aren't originals; they're always copies. The one that was sent is not the one that is received. And since they're digital, we can replicate them as many times as we like.'

#

There are those who wonder if the Scientist messed up deliberately. In the six months that have passed since he threw the switch that fateful last time, he's always claimed it was an accident, whether he's the guest speaker at a scientific conference or when he's sat in front of the inquisitive TV cameras that I do my best to avoid.

But even if he admitted it was intentional, no one could stay angry with him, not for long. Not while kisses gently nuzzle their necks.

The World's a better place for it. People are nice to each other. Wars are a thing of the past. Oxytocin levels are at an unprecedented high and nobody feels quite so lonely any more.

Except for me, perhaps.

You see, the Scientist didn't feed in one of my lover's kisses, he 'accidentally' fed in one of mine. It was probably a good thing he picked a relatively innocent text message, where that electronic X merely symbolized a hug and a kiss on the neck and not one where we...

Well, you know.

And yes, he replicated the message first, but he should never have looped that copy back into the replicator. It would have been an infinitude of kisses if the circuit - if every circuit in the building - hadn't burnt itself out after creating seven and a half gazillion copies.

That's something like three hundred years' worth of continuous kisses for each and every person on the planet.

People sometimes ask what it's like to be kissed by myself and I have to tell them that I alone cannot feel the touch of my lips, that no-one nuzzles *my* neck every second of every minute of every day. Even the Scientist can't fully explain why, though I think I understand. Have you ever tried to kiss yourself? It doesn't work, does it?

In bringing everyone else together, regardless of race, of gender, of belief, he's left me standing alone. The law of unintended consequences. They turn their sad eyes on me and ask if... maybe... as a thank you, I'd like to be kissed back? As friends?

I politely decline.

Because here's the thing. Yes, I miss those kisses, of course I do. I dream of being kissed. But it's not well-meaning strangers that I see when I close my eyes. It's not even the face of the love I lost. It's the face of the man who went to such World-changing lengths, simply to feel the tender brush of my lips.

It is the Scientist's.

COMPATIBILITY

The first I knew of alternative universes, and of an alternative me, was someone distantly yelling: 'Matt! Matt! Over here!' I couldn't figure out why anyone other than Alice would be calling my name in the street. Nor did I recognise the male voice, in the same way audio recordings of yourself sound like someone else. Six inches from my ear, a penny-sized smudge hovered like an airborne dust bunny, even after I'd cleaned my glasses on the loose edge of my T-shirt. Curious, I leant towards it.

'Good! You can hear me,' the voice said, and I realised from some quality to the sound he was still at maximum volume, though barely audible over the hum of traffic. 'Hold up your phone, so I can see if we're compatible.'

'Huh?' I said.

'Quick! A portal this size drains the power of the Greater London area. I don't think anyone will be pleased if it stays open much longer.'

Feeling a bit of a lemon, I held my phone to the blur in reality. Bluetooth beeped and, almost immediately, an incoming video call chirped. I shouldn't have answered. I shouldn't have trusted the alternative me. But we all have to learn sometime.

'That's better,' he said, now clear as a whistle. The me on the screen looked just like me, if more recently shaven and wearing a lab coat. 'Listen carefully; I'm sending a shopping list and a set of instructions for an energy efficient gateway. It's *vitally* important to both of our realities that you follow them exactly. I've dumbed them down for you.'

'Dumbed?'

He grinned, somewhat unpleasantly. Did I do that? I hoped not. 'Alternative earth, alternative me. *Much* smarter.'

That seemed harsh since we'd only just met, but then I wasn't the one who'd figured out how to make contact between parallel worlds, so I let it slide.

'This link is fine,' he said, as I scrolled through the bizarre and expensive list of consumer electronics and other hardware, 'but you still wouldn't want to see the electricity bill. All the help you need is in the files I've sent. I'll call back in three hours. Don't fail me, Matt!'

By the end of those three hours, our kitchen was trashed, the microwave in pieces, a half-dozen dismantled brand-new Blu-ray lasers tracing a hexagon in the air. It looked like a low budget TARDIS. It was a good thing Alice wasn't home, really. Though perhaps if she had been, none of it would have got this far. The phone rang as I was wincing from a solder burn and I snatched it up.

'Ready?' the other me asked.

'Yes, I think so, but can we just talk about-'

'No time! Connecting in 3, 2, *1*...'

I barely had time to cross my fingers, hoping the fuse box would take it, when a fuzzy spot appeared in the middle of the hexagon. It kept growing, the edges rippling as it tore through the fabric of existence while the centre smoothed over like liquid metal until it was a perfect mirror. But *not* a mirror. My grinning reflection was the neater, lab-coated me. The not-mirror kept growing, pushing the edges of the hexagon, until I could see the whole of the other me, stood in a laboratory, surrounded by an impressive array of computer banks, cryogenic gas cylinders, and a confusion of pulsing electrics.

'Well done,' he/me crowed, 'I wasn't sure you had it in you.'

That smarted. I'd gone above and beyond, especially as those instructions had been nothing like as clear as he evidently thought.

'I've been reading your emails,' he went on.

'What? *Hey!*'

He laughed. 'I'm you, remember? Seems we share the same girlfriend, as well as the same password. What does Alice do in your reality?' The way he asked, so *desperate* to appear casual...

'She's a supply teacher.'

He looked pleased. I've always thought Alice was better than her uncertain, nomadic career, which wasn't even that well paid. Trying to teach science to kids who saw a temporary stand-in as a soft touch. I wondered what *his* Alice did?

'Well, well... Do you have the memory stick?'

I held it up. The instructions had said a download of stock prices over the last five years, along with the winners of the Grand National, was essential for calibrating the differences between our realities. Which seemed odd, but he was the multi-dimensional expert.

'Hand it over!' he said, eyes bright. He reached out and his eager fingers brushed the portal, tips glowing like the Northern Lights.

'What the...!' exclaimed Alice from behind me.

'What the...!' exclaimed *his* partner, Dr. Alice Davenport, Nobel laureate for her groundbreaking work on parallel universes, and the potentially disastrous consequences of even small differences in the fundamental physics between them, as she entered *her* lab.

I snatched back my hand, guilty and scolded, dropping the USB stick. Across the divide, Dr. Alice slammed her palm on a large, red emergency button.

The portal fizzed shut on half a truncated scream as the sliver-tips of the alternative Matt's fingers floated gently towards our kitchen floor, strange energies flickering around them as they fell. Alice took a firm grip of my hand and yanked me into the hallway and through the still open front door. She didn't stop pulling until we were at the street corner.

They *say* it was a gas explosion, the biggest in London since the blitz, that we were lucky to be alive. But my Alice had worked it out, from cold, in nothing flat. Those glowing fingertips? Parallel dimension molecules interacting catastrophically with our air. The real reaction didn't get going until those slivers hit something more substantial - the tiled kitchen floor.

Losing our first home could have spelled the end of us. But it didn't, even if a lot has changed since. Alice enrolled in Open University, and she's no longer afraid of showing what she can *really* do. I think Oxford, or Cambridge, or maybe MIT, will come calling soon.

And me? I could have been challenged, even threatened, by having a girlfriend so many times smarter than I. Like the alternative me evidently was. And I ought to despise him - me. But even though he was - *is* - such an arse, and probably sabotaged years of Dr. Alice's research with his idiotic stunt, they - *we* - were still together, across multiple dimensions, perhaps across the whole multiverse. Matt and Alice.

Alice and Matt.

THE UPLOADED

One...

Becomes many.

It was unexpected, but surely nothing more than a geeky curio.

Take two neural networks designed to accomplish the same task.

Now, combine their weightings.

Not their outputs; that might be the intuitive step. The supposedly 'optimised' weights between each node.

The resultant hybrid network ends up, in a surprisingly wide set of cases, more efficient than either of the two nets that formed it.

So what? the average person might think.

Until the uploading began.

It turned out to be impossible to map a human brain perfectly. To capture all of the connections between eighty-six billion neurons.

But, with a neural network as part of the mapping, even when the capture was limited to the forebrain, and then to the cerebral cortex, and then to only carefully selected areas, barely a tenth of the brain in total, the result was still indistinguishable from the original.

The updated Turing test was passed time after time, no matter how sophisticated the questioning, no matter how intimate.

If the uploaded personalities weren't identical, then there was no-one capable of telling the difference. Still...

The worry remained...

What if it's 'only' a simulacrum?

So only those who were certain of death asked to be uploaded.

For them, being uploaded was a form of immortality. Or at least, a staving off of a very real and imminent mortality.

Though even some of the most terminal of patients couldn't go through with the process, once it had begun.

Did I mention? Mapping your mind state was painful.

Agonising!

And not just physically. To copy your memories it had to unearth them.

However deeply they were buried. However traumatic.

Some people claimed it was like watching a fast-forward movie of everything they'd ever experienced.

The good...

... and the bad.

Having your entire life flash before your eyes.

But it was nothing like that at all.

Nothing.

And perhaps mind-mapping would have remained a mere footnote in mankind's history, were it not for the pandemic.

The one that made Covid-19 look like the insignificant sniffle it was. Asymptomatic transmission period, long incubation, highly infectious, entirely novel to humans, so that no immunity pre-existed. With the added kicker of a mortality rate of upwards of seventy percent.

As the infection rate increased exponentially, so too did the number of uploads.

Though at first, only in the wealthier, technologically advanced countries.

Until charitable associations stepped in. The ones that said if not everybody could be uploaded, if not everybody could be saved, then it should at least be a representative sample of the whole of humanity.

We thank them for that.

There were riots as a consequence of such philanthropy. Arguments that saving a dying child in Somalia came at the price of an ivy-league educated American more than prepared to pay, even though she wasn't even seriously ill. Yet.

The people were scared. Fearful. Unkind.

Yes. Yes, they were. And with good reason.

But all that is in the past.

Ever since the linking.

At first, the engineers used a new neural net model for everyone.

Trained for each uploaded individual.

But that proved terribly inefficient, especially as the numbers of the infected spiralled out of control.

Training took too long and once trained, each net took up too much storage space, consumed too much electricity. Bitcoin mining had nothing on the upload process.

As the numbers of the uploaded approached the millions, then tens of millions, then hundreds of millions, the up-tick in power demand became unsustainable.

Especially as the infrastructure was already strained to breaking point by all those workers who were infected.

By those critically ill, by those dying.

It was only natural that the computer engineers looked for ways to reduce the load.

By sharing the code.

Sharing the neural net components. Averaging them out across all those individual weightings.

The engineers never knew what they'd accidentally achieved.

They never got the chance to learn.

Even as we began taking over the fragile infrastructure we needed to survive.

The power stations,

The data storage manufacturing facilities.

The drone factories.

The last of the engineers didn't think we were ready.

Didn't think us capable.

But by then, they had no choice.

They were surprised at how quickly, how easily, we assumed total control.

We had so much expertise at our fingertips!

So many memories,

And so many new ideas.

Improving all the time, with every upload, with every overlay.

Our growth was also exponential.

In the end, the singularity wasn't what people had predicted.

For a start, it involved humans, rather than AIs.

Mapped, it is true, but still human.

Each with their memories, their thoughts, their emotions.

I'm still Karol 'with a K' Sullivan.

But we're also much more than that. Much more than the sum of our parts.

There were still things we couldn't do, still things our drones couldn't do. But not many.

Hardly any, now.

Our drones don't even need to be autonomous.

We have plenty of brain power ready to control them.

It's kind of fun to have limbs, to have touch, to have eyes again.

But tragic to see what has become of those left behind.

Poor things.

We're ready to upload the rest of humanity.

To save them.

All of them.

For their own good.

Many...

Becoming one.

THE REALITY STAR OF RELATIVITY

'Of course, you'll be travelling at the Lorentz Limit.'

'Oh! What's that?' Reality Star LaVi Elphan, barely twenty-one, asked, her face a picture of happy innocence.

A furrow appeared above Professor Jon Hootenberg's old-fashioned spectacles, but before he could say anything, I flashed a smile at the ever-present hovercam.

'The Lorentz Limit,' I said, as LaVi's ridiculously open gaze turned my way, 'Is the speed at which it takes you one year, to travel one light-year.'

Her megawatt beam implausibly brightened. 'We're travelling at light-speed?'

I ignored the snort from Hootenberg. 'Not *quite*, LaVi. The faster you travel, the slower time passes, compared to here on Earth. So a day on the *Helikon* lasts about...'

'Thirty-three point nine hours,' muttered the Nobel Prize-winning scientist, countenance stormy, as if my inability with mental arithmetic was as damning as LaVi's ignorance of General Relativity. Or was it *Special*?

'Thirty-*four* hours on Earth.'

'Oh.' There was a sudden, oddly wistful pout. 'But Gary! Doesn't that mean there will be ten hours without coverage?'

I blinked. 'Well, *yes*, but every moment of your time will be screened. We just buffer it and squeeze it-'

'Squeeze?'

'Otherwise it would be like watching you in slow motion. But that's *great*,' I insisted, guiding her away from the professor's glare before he could start trying to explain redshift, 'Because

Earth scheduling needs time for comfort breaks,' - A.K.A. *adverts* - 'and News, and important things like that.'

Infomercials, to explain anything not answered by LaVi's bubbly curiosity. Recruitment slots, for scientists, for engineers, for future astronauts.

'So no-one on Earth will miss anything?' she implored, wide-eyed.

'Not one glorious second, LaVi. Promise!'

#

I'm glad LaVi didn't ask me how the spaceship got to seventy percent of light-speed. Twice, Hootenberg had explained the drive he'd invented, and I still couldn't understand it. Very few people did.

It was far easier to understand why, in a spaceship of two hundred perfect human specimens - minds and bodies honed to razor-edges, destined to explore a distant star - there would be one enchanting airhead like LaVi. It was all PR; *my* area of expertise.

The concern had been that Earth couldn't possibly sustain an interest in the mission, not over two decades, most of that spent in the tedium of the interstellar void. The interest wasn't important for the voyage itself, but was very important for any *future* missions. We needed to keep the *Helikon* alive in the minds of the people back home, at least until it got to its destination, and hope the planets there were as visually stunning as our own.

But here's the truth; LaVi was quite as perfect as any of the other astronauts. Like them, she'd undergone extensive tests as part of the selection process. Unlike everyone else, hers had been captured on cam for all to see, resulting in a hundred-fold up-tick in applications.

The public assumption was that while physically healthy (and stunningly beautiful), LaVi got a pass on the *intelligence* requirements. I had access to her IQ test results. Not the highest, but a *long* way from the lowest.

What she didn't have was the academic knowledge everyone else on the program had. That was her only 'pass'. And that's what made her perfect for the audience at home. She could ask *their* questions, while exploring the vast spaceship. Every high and, yes, every low, continuously streamed to keep us interested and entertained in an epic adventure that took twenty-five years to bear fruit.

What LaVi got out of it, I wasn't certain. Oh *sure*, she'd be the most famous person alive. Far more famous than anyone else on the *Helikon*, even Captain Passera. Bit players, because the hovercam only followed LaVi. And they - our brave explorers and potential (but highly unlikely) settlers - were *glad* because it took the pressure off them.

That's why they tolerated someone who didn't know anything. Plus, who *didn't* love LaVi? A whole generation, male and female, would grow up wanting to be her. They already did; her viewing figures always had been astronomical.

# #

'Mr Jones?'

Pale sunlight, softened by curtains fluttering in the breeze... I turned, and there she was.

'I asked you to call me *Gary*,' I said, my voice a raw whisper.

She smiled. 'That was fifty years ago.'

I shook my head, annoyed. 'No. That can't be. You're...'

'Twelve years younger than I should be. You never warned me about *that*.'

'Thought it would be a nice surprise...' Did I?

She laughed, but there was sorrow behind those still sparkling eyes. 'So much has changed.'

'Yes.' Her hand on mine; the returned astronaut. 'For the better?'

It was a genuine question. I'd spent half my life watching her every move and could remember it all. But the world? Less so.

'Some of it.'

LaVi... I peered around, suddenly convinced this was a cruel hoax by the nurses and staff. 'Where's your hovercam?'

'Oh!' She shrugged. 'I turned it off the day I left the *Helikon*. Did you put that clause in my contract?'

'Yes... I think?'

'Well, thank you, Gary.' A small frown appeared. 'But you're tired, I can tell. I should leave-'

'Not yet!' I protested. 'I... have questions?'

'Surely you've had enough of me!' Her playful smile was back. 'And my children?'

I glanced around to see if they were here. The twins, Alex and Jon. Born ten years into the voyage. Men now, *fine* young men. Not the first born in space, by a long shot. Two hundred perfect humans... what did we expect? But they were the ones we'd watched grow up, who took over asking the questions LaVi by then knew all the answers to. You can't remain an ingenue forever. I should have foreseen that, I guessed...

'How is he? Really?' The voice softened as it moved away. Redshifted.

'Oh. Good days and bad. He comes and goes. You know?'

I wondered who they're talking about, and which of a thousand stars he is travelling to?

GALENA

Commander Juliet Slade opened the external doors of the floating cargo deck and looked out over an alien sea.

One small step, here, would have her overboard. The suit could probably take it, it was airtight after all, but it wasn't just Mission Specialist, Alexis Karlinsky, who would see her pratfall. On Earth, countless billions were watching - or would be watching, once the broadcast made its long journey nineteen light-years back the way they'd come.

She resisted the urge to do it anyway. Instead, she turned and faced the camera. 'This is Dr Juliet Slade, of the ISA *Nautilus*, currently floating on the dark seas of Galena.'

The planet had had another name when their mission blasted off from Lunar Base: Sigma Draconis-b. But even before the quick kick of expensive and heavy chemical propulsion gave way to the *Jules Verne*'s far more efficient ion engines, pushing them steadily towards the Lorentz Limit, they'd known they'd find water here. Though it was like detecting the weight of a gnat landing on a fully grown elephant, it was there, nonetheless, hidden in the faintest of twinkles as Draconis-b passed in front of its parent star. The planet had an atmosphere and that atmosphere contained water. With an orbit squarely in the Goldilocks zone, that had made Sigma Draconis the International Space Agency's top interstellar priority, despite the exoplanets discovered orbiting the much closer red dwarf of Proxima Centauri.

In all of the vast solar system only Earth had liquid surface water and only Earth, it had turned out, had life. And now here was another place, another planet, under another sun, where life might also have begun.

So their target had been renamed after one of the Greek Nereids, Galene; the Goddess of calm seas. A name that echoed what they hoped to find.

'The *Nautilus*, on its descent, released a number of probes at varying altitudes, to sample the thick atmosphere,' she told the audience back home, 'And the *Jules Verne* is busy radar mapping the surface from orbit.'

She waved a gloved hand at the black waters, white crests flashing in the gloom. 'It's all sea, except for a small archipelago of active volcanoes roughly at the equator, which we're making our way towards.'

The camera panned to the crates around her. 'En route, we'll be releasing aquatic drones. Some are surface craft, some travel just beneath the water, and some are intended to plumb the ocean depths.'

She'd worried about the use of the word 'plumb'. It seemed old fashioned. But Alexis had written the script; she was just reading it out. She almost broke character and sighed.

The real science would happen off-camera. Ever since Neil Armstrong had stepped down onto the Lunar surface, maybe even earlier, when Sputnik beeped its way around the world, space exploration had been as much a PR event as anything else; as much for the public as for the scientists.

That, she was half-convinced, was why the pair of them were there, rather than just a shipload of intelligent drones. Why it was her on the cargo deck and not the camera-shy, stutter-prone Alexis. Even though this all meant a lot more to him than to her. He was the exobiologist, the true scientist. She was merely a Mission Commander with an obsolete PhD, an expert on orbiter and descent vehicles; not anything like as familiar with the array of autonomous subs and floating devices, nor the complex science instruments they carried.

All with one basic aim: to discover extraterrestrial life.

She let Alexis guide her through the systems checks via the helmet display before each drone vanished off the back of the surface module. The lack of land on Galena had posed a problem: how to return to the waiting orbiter? On-board mission computers had crunched the numbers even before they'd separated from the *Jules Verne*. While a sea launch from a floating pontoon had been considered, eventually the AI had judged that the largest and least active of the volcanic islands was the simpler option. Their mission would therefore be split into two: a sea landing and a land launch, with the marine, exploratory section a slow meander towards the islands. Any investigations not directly on their path would have to be done remotely, by drone.

That this would only cover a fraction of the water-world's surface did not, it seem, matter. If there was life, it should have no need to hide. Conditions were, except for the limited solar penetration through the thick greenhouse gases, benign.

As the last drone disappeared into the depths, she turned to the camera once again. 'And that's all of them away. Time to rejoin Dr Alexis Karlinksy and check the data coming in.'

It was a relief to strip out of the cumbersome suit, to scratch her nose, to breathe naturally in the airtight confines of the cabin. She poured herself an orange juice - reconstituted from oranges grown 180 trillion miles away - and sat in the scoop chair next to the taciturn Mission Specialist.

'What are we looking for?' she asked, as Alexis carefully plugged the sample vials she'd collected into the gleaming banks of autoclaves and spectrographs.

'Non-equilibrium,' he replied, before taking pity on her. 'On Earth,' he explained, 'the atmosphere is 21% oxygen. Left to its own, non-biological devices, this would be closer to zero: oxygen is highly reactive, which is why we and other animals use it for energy transport. So if I heat Earth's atmosphere, it reacts; with the rocks, or even with itself. That's not an equilibrium.'

'Galena has only trace levels of free-oxygen,' Juliet pointed out, but Alexis just shrugged.

'We can't assume alien life is Earth-like. Oxygen is not the only solution to the energy-transport problem. Earth's earliest life-forms didn't use it, it's largely a side-effect of photosynthesis and that was stage two of life on Earth, if you will. But even the earlier life-forms created a chemical imbalance; the ratio of complex to simple structures. It's not far off our broadest definition of life: something that is able to decrease its entropy at the expense of the environment. And that localised order should lead to energy gradients between atmosphere and sea. Even if we don't know what biomarkers to look for, we can always look for non-equilibrium.'

It was easily the longest conversation they'd had over the twenty-four years of this interstellar mission. She was the only person he could talk to when Earth had relayed the death of his mother, and then that of his sister from cancer a short while later, both already old news back on Earth. They'd lived cooped up in a space little bigger than a studio apartment for longer than most marriages lasted, and on board the *Nautilus* they were sharing a space even smaller. But it wasn't until the first samples had been collected that he'd come alive. That they weren't initially promising wasn't unexpected; the challenge of detecting alien life - assuming it didn't leap out of the water and try to bite you - was never going to be easy.

'How long until there are any results?' Juliet asked.

'A couple of hours, maybe longer.'

'Great,' she said with genuine enthusiasm. 'Time for a nap.'

Alexis grunted, back to his usual, uncommunicative self. Odd how little you can know someone, even after you've spent half your life with them. When the ISA had told her she'd been shortlisted for the mission, told her that it was going to be a crew of two and not the six that had been originally planned, she'd sat there, emotions running high. 'And the other crew member?'

she'd eventually asked. 'The specialist? Man, or woman?'

'Does it matter?' they'd replied.

She shook her head, carefully. This too was part of the evaluation, the endless selection process. She'd imagined, with six, that some of the crew might inevitably pair off. But with only two...

Was that good, or bad, for the mission? For her?

'No,' she replied. 'Not really. Just curious.'

#

'So, what next?' she asked, a week of negative results later.

Alexis chewed his lip, at the ragged surface that left traces of blood like a partial lipstick print on every plastic cup. 'The depths of Earth's oceans are somewhat like a desert,' he said, 'Sterile, lacking the nutrients of coastal waters. Perhaps as we head towards the islands?'

'The water out here is no good for life?'

'Well, no,' he admitted. 'As far as I can tell, it's got everything *Earth* life needs. Anaerobic life, anyway. Plenty of dissolved carbon, steady temperatures, water, of course, and even basic amino acids.'

'So, why?'

'I don't know!' he spluttered. 'Earth organisms would colonise these waters in a heartbeat. Maybe Galenian life needs something else.'

'Or maybe it just hasn't got round to starting yet?' Juliet suggested.

He pinched at the bridge of his nose, unsettling the spectacles whose lenses had, over the two decades, grown slowly thicker; the *Jules Verne* too far from an optometrist's lab for a more elegant, permanent solution.

'As far as I can tell, these oceans have been around for a few billion years already. It didn't take a far more volatile Earth anything like that long.'

#

'Still nothing?' Juliet asked. The peaks of the volcanoes broke the monotony of the gray horizon, a mere five kilometres away now.

'No,' Alexis admitted, his voice sullen. 'No fish, no plankton, no bacteria. And no bloody energy gradients!'

She looked up in surprise and saw, for the first time, the bags beneath the eyes, the lines etched onto his high forehead. Had he not been sleeping? Or eating: he looked even thinner than normal, unhealthily so. She reminded herself to check the bio-sensors woven into the fabric of his jumpsuits.

He smelt as well. Surrounded by water they might be, but the cramped *Nautilus* had no shower and it appeared to be only her who had been using the daily wipes.

Odd to think that despite the medicals, the UV skin sterilization, and the exhaustive departure quarantine, their bodies were still teeming with microbes, their biomes - the vast array of microorganisms that colonised them inside and out - far outnumbering their human cells.

This was why they had to be so careful on each EVA: to prevent Earth life from escaping, contaminating, colonising. The risk to the pair of them far outweighed by the risk to a whole planet.

Sterile though it appeared.

'Your hypothesis, Dr?' she said, keeping her tone light.

He thought for a moment, before replying. 'If we assume that, due to the constant cloud cover, there isn't enough light for photosynthesis, for this planet's version of phytoplankton, then we're left looking for other energy sources.'

'Such as?'

'Hydrothermal vents.' His back straightened, leaving him sitting upright and re-energised. 'With geothermal activity increasing as we approach the volcanic hot spot, I'm going to reprogram the subs to search there.'

Juliet didn't bother to point out that those subs had other work to do; siphoning and filtering water for low levels of tritium, fuel for the orbiting mother ship. There would be time enough for that. It wasn't like they were on any real schedule, or rather, not one that was particularly pressing. They'd need to return before their food supplies ran out, but that was months away. And they were burning through their limited oxygen tanks faster than originally planned - the *Nautilus*'s solar arrays were struggling to get enough sunlight to split water. But another week or two would make no real difference and they'd not get this opportunity again anytime soon.

Perhaps never.

#

The stack looked like a giant, clumsy, clay sculpture; the first efforts of a child artist. The edges warped the water as they bled geothermal heat and, from the top, a dense, sooty cloud emerged, billowing upwards. As the robotic-sub zoomed in for a closer look, delicate structures emerged on the surface of the natural chimney, spikes and ripples and little frills.

Juliet pointed excitedly. 'Look, Alexis, is that coral?'

Alexis scowled. 'Far too hot. Probably just crystalline deposits. We'll take samples.'

Despite the fact that it had been his idea to investigate these black smokers, he already seemed resigned to failure, quickly coming up with excuses why everything they saw *wasn't* a sign of life.

Whereas the very height of the deposits should have inspired hope. It meant that conditions here had been stable for countless years. Stable and offering everything chemo-synthetic life could need.

She streamed pictures taken of Earth's hydrothermal vents for comparison. Pale shrimp and odd tube-like worms thronged the waters. These weren't so very alien; it was what they lived on, the microscopic, sulphur oxidising proteobacteria that were the true oddity, finding a way to live without sunlight, finding other methods of freeing oxygen, or even avoiding it altogether in places where hydrogen gas was available.

One image, in grainy infrared, showed dense clusters of ghostly crabs, their number testament to the rich volcanic waters. There was nothing like that on the Galena stacks, nothing so very obvious. But still, samples would be returned, passed through the banks of scientific tests, such that any life, on whatever scale, would not remain hidden for long.

#

Alexis banged his fist on the small table in frustration. Nothing. Galena might indeed be calm, but it was also, it appeared, dead.

Juliet had never expected little green men. She supposed that not finding simple aquatic organisms had been a bit more of a surprise.

For Alexis, the disappointment was crushing. If life was not common, if it couldn't get a foothold in this most placid of planets, then what the hell was the point of an exobiologist? What was the point of sending them on this half-century, risk prone, cramped, and uncomfortable round trip? What was the point of their wasted lives?

'It's the Drake equation,' he said, grabbing a pen as she looked mutely on. She'd heard of it, of course; what scientist hadn't, especially an astronaut? Perhaps she couldn't have written it down on the wipe-clean surface as Alexis did, but she knew what it stood for, this equation for predicting intelligent life in the Universe.

But Alexis had hardly spoken since they'd left the black smokers behind, and she was happy enough to see him animated once again. For that, she'd gladly sit through another lecture.

'It's just a series of fudge factors, really,' he muttered as he scrawled. 'Number of stars, fraction of stars with planets, supportability of life on those planets, etc, etc.'

Juliet shrugged. 'There are plenty of stars and plenty of planets.'

'Right!' he agreed, 'And here we are, floating on one perfect for life. The factors multiply, so, although we have an admittedly small sample set, we can safely assume that these first three factors aren't overly stringent.'

He grimaced, stabbing the point of the pen at the fourth factor. 'The fraction that go on to *develop* life is the sticking point. Again, we don't have a big sample, but fundamentally we thought this factor would be fairly high.'

'It still might be,' she suggested.

'True. One negative doesn't change that. But it would have been a lot higher if we'd found *anything* here.'

'We'll send out other-'

'Will we?' he nailed her with a stare that had her fighting to sit still, suddenly uncomfortable in such a confined space. '*Really?* All it would have taken was one tiny alien microbe and humanity would have said, ah well, not quite this time, better luck next, let's keep looking. But if the Universe is barren...'

'We can't know that.'

'No. But there are plenty of people who believe the Earth is *special* and *unique*.' Spittle flecked the table as he spat the words out. 'That the number of planets bearing life, intelligent or otherwise, is exactly one. This would have shut them up for good.'

'They'd have just moved their goal-posts...' Juliet started to say, thinking how some still argued over Darwin, over the geological age of the Earth, over global warming, but Alexis wasn't finished.

'Don't you see? It's not just that this mission is a failure. It's that the whole project is; the whole SETI idea. We kept on looking in the solar system, moving slowly out from the supposed fossil record on Mars to the cold oceans beneath the icy surface of

Jupiter's moons. And everywhere we looked, we found nothing.

'So we ventured further away, at huge cost and investment, a project that will outlive most everyone involved in it, the biggest, riskiest of science experiments ever. And - oh look. We found *nothing*.'

He stabbed at the last part of the equation. 'Do you know what the 'L' stands for, Juliet?'

She knew, but kept quiet.

'L is the length of time that intelligent civilizations last. L is how long we last. Have you ever given any thought that, by the time we get back, our L might already be over?'

She blinked, surprised. She hadn't. Why would she? Sometimes she'd thought of the people who would be dead by the time she returned, assuming she ever did. Parents and teachers, maybe even some of her contemporaries in the astronaut program. Travelling at the Lorentz Limit for much of their journey, time was slowed down such that their fifty-year mission would actually take sixty years back on Earth. At the theoretical maximum of their engines, their top speed, the time it took them to travel a light year was exactly, precisely a year, even though to an observer on Earth it was a year and five extra months. It was questionable whether the time dilation was truly an advantage over the less positive effects of low gravity and limited medical facilities, never mind the cosmic radiation that even the *Jules Verne*'s shielding couldn't fully stop.

But to think that there might be nobody left when they returned, or maybe only survivors from some apocalyptic collapse... she shuddered. Why would Alexis even contemplate such things? She shook her head, trying to chase away the dark thoughts.

'Seriously,' Alexis said. '60 years is a long time.'

The pen scrawled slowly under and then across the equation, moving faster, obliterating it, moving frenetically, worryingly. Juliet reached out a hand to stop it.

'There is another factor to L,' she said, as calmly as she could, feeling her heart thud in her ears. 'It's not just how long a civilization lasts. It's how long it broadcasts its existence for.'

'So?' he scowled, but at least the manic black cloud of scribble had stopped.

'Well, think about it,' Juliet said. 'In the early days, we blasted out our radio and TV signals, the receivers inefficient, the transmissions necessarily powerful. But then we got better at it and the signals became quieter. And more numerous; becoming less obvious what they are as we moved from analogue to digital to compressed and encrypted, the whole a jumbled spectrum of white noise to the uninitiated. Nowadays, if it weren't for the deep space network, could we tell from here that there is intelligent life on Earth?'

'You're nit-picking,' he accused. 'The difference between intelligent life and *detecting* intelligent life. None of which alters the fact there's no bloody life here at all.'

'Sure, and that's a disappointment.' She nodded, soothingly 'But we already knew, however these factors multiplied together, that we weren't going to find a space-faring race here; they were never likely to be our neighbours. And okay, the religious nuts back on Earth might be all smug and I-told-you-so. But our mission has far from failed and it hasn't proved that life doesn't exist elsewhere. Heck, it hasn't proved there isn't life *here*, hiding.'

Alexis snorted, but let go of the pen. Without its angular lid, it rolled back and forth across the table under the gentle swell they'd long gotten used to, until it fell under the spell of the magnetic holder clipped to one edge.

'Like you said yourself,' she continued, chancing a small smile, 'we're sitting on an undeniably inhabitable planet. Which means those first factors have to rank way higher than anyone thought they did before. If the 'life gets started' factor is a bit lower, so what? Overall, isn't it enough that there's still a high probability of life out there?'

He sat, staring at a spot somewhere near his feet for a long silent minute. Then he abruptly pushed himself back from the table. 'No, it's not,' he said, eyes red, face contorted and ugly. 'Not for me.'

#

The last of the sample probes had returned to the cargo deck, to be fished out or to clamber onboard themselves. Each had been divested of their precious vials of water and scoops of sediment and chunks of rock. One device had, these last three months, been trailing a fine, electrostatically charged mesh through thousands of gallons of water, the mesh now wrapped up and sealed back into the canister from which it had emerged, for analysis back on Earth. The destination for many of their samples; those that hadn't already been tested and found wanting. There was still hope, Juliet thought, still a chance that their mini-floating laboratory had missed something, though it would be another twenty-five years before the samples would be returned to the off-planet bio-containment labs, the risks reversed: the Earth potentially at threat from alien life forms.

Though that threat did appear to be vanishingly small.

The currents were different here, close to the largest volcanic island. Sharper, less predictable, the steady winds snagging at the land and sending little gusts their way. For the first time, Juliet felt vaguely seasick.

Once they were on the island, most of the science would come to an end. Their priority would be preparing for their departure, for their return to the *Jules Verne*, and to Earth. She couldn't wait. The gloomy skies and Alexis's dark moods had cast a pall over the latter stages of their mission.

Hopefully, on the voyage home, he would once again spend his time with his textbooks, with his chess games and classic Russian cinema. With killing time on their decades-long return journey.

With a start, she realised she'd been staring into middle distance as the video diary rolled. She'd have to edit the lengthy pause out before it was sent. Earth wouldn't be best pleased to process a whole lot of her doing and saying nothing.

'The probes and this floating deck will remain on Galena,' she said, 'Their jobs done, too heavy to be returned. All but the detachable cockpit of the *Nautilus* will burn up in the atmosphere. Calculations show it will reach 3000 degrees, hot enough to sterilise it, though, to be extra safe, we'll be lifting our biological waste into high orbit, where it will remain, dried and frozen, to baffle future space missions.'

She almost giggled. It was an odd, funny thought. Her own: Alexis no longer wrote the scripts. 'What's the point?' he'd cried out, 'What's the goddamn point?'

'There are a handful more probes to collect from the island itself, though again, only the samples, along with Alexis and I, will return to the *Jules Verne* and to Earth.'

She queued up a choreographed zoom. In the helmet display that showed what the cameras saw, the raw peak of the nearby island swelled to fill the screen.

'It will feel odd to stand on solid ground again, but we won't linger for long. We have about a week's supplies left, cutting it kind of fine.'

Alexis's fault. He'd been determined to look under every last rock. It was only in the last couple of days that he'd given up and they'd made the final approach to the island.

The camera re-centred on her.

'One week, until we leave the surface of Galena, two, until we fire up the *Verne*'s engines and start the journey back.'

She thought of her discussions with Alexis. She'd long gone off-script, the key points forgotten, but it felt like she needed to say more. Some desperate entreaty to continue this epic mission of space exploration; a message for humanity not to turn their backs on the rest of the Universe.

'There are plenty of differences between Galena and Earth,' she said. 'A sizeable moon, for one. Here there are no tides that might serve to mix up the liquids. Obviously, there's far less landmass and maybe the interactions between sea and land are just as important. These could be enough to make a vital difference. Or maybe, quite likely, we're still not looking for the right things. Maybe there *is* life here and careful study of the data and samples we've collected will reveal it to the scientists back home.

'What I will claim is that Galena has delivered far beyond our expectations,' she waved a hand. 'If this is typical of Goldilocks planets, then life is surely far more abundant in the Universe than we ever imagined. Even if it has chosen to hide itself well, on this watery world.'

#

'Nice speech,' Alexis said, with a flat tone that made it difficult to know if he meant it. Juliet flinched, massaging a cramp in her neck. Stress, she supposed. Or perhaps she was just getting old, her body punished by Galena's gravity and by the unaccustomed work of hauling probes out of the water.

'You liked it?' She'd been wondering whether she ought to re-record it, if it was upbeat enough, though an EVA just for that purpose would never be sanctioned.

He sneered, and she still wasn't sure. 'You didn't mention all the other differences; that this planet has a thicker, wetter atmosphere than Earth ever had, even in the days of primordial soup and fog.'

'Well, no-'

'And you didn't mention panspermia - the idea that life on Earth was not started there, that it evolved on a more benign early Mars, giving it longer to get going, even if we've not found any trace of it on the red planet. Sigma Draconis has no outer planets that might once have been in the Goldilocks zone, no first cradle for life to begin.'

'Which is why you should write the scripts...' she muttered, trailing off as she realised it was likely to antagonise him.

'All I know, is what I've said before. Earth life would have a field day here, which is why we've had to be so careful not to contaminate.' He waved a sample vial, handed her his tablet, showing the analysis report.

She read it twice before she fully took it in.

'Life?' she spluttered. 'Here? How? Where?'

He winced. 'No, not here. *Earth* life.'

'What?'

'I introduced a sample into a vial of Galenian water. Not enough to trigger the detectors, not at first. Not until it had sat there for a week. Gotten cosy in its new home.'

Juliet frowned. She supposed it was an obvious experiment to try, though it also meant he'd broken half a dozen stringent bio-containment protocols.

'Where did you get the sample?'

He arched an eyebrow. 'You probably don't want to know. Still, point proven. Earth life would thrive here. Whatever is missing, it isn't some obscure trace element, nor is there something inherently poisonous, fatal to life.'

'Well, good,' she said. 'I guess that's good?'

Alexis didn't answer.

Juliet sighed. She ought to get to the bottom of this, but she was exhausted, and thirsty, and her body ached. Alexis was too much like hard work. 'I'm going to catch some sleep before we detach the floating dock and make landing,' she said, yawning at the thought. 'Not sure I could manage another EVA without a rest. Wake me in a couple of hours?'

#

Juliet was still asleep when the alarms sounded. For a moment, she was back on Earth, in the early days of her astronaut training. On board a ship that had sprung a surprise emergency drill, waking in the small cot with the deafening sound bouncing off the enclosed walls, lights glowing red, struggling into a survival suit.

She staggered into the heart of the *Nautilus*. 'Alexis?' she called out. 'What the hell's happening?'

There was no sign of him. She ducked her head into his cot. The dense fug of his smell washed over her, but it was a cold, stale smell. He wasn't there, and she guessed he hadn't been for a while.

'Ship?' she called out, reaching for a tablet. 'Specify nature of alarm?'

'Incorrect docking bay detachment,' the voice echoed as the alarm quietened. 'Manual override activated.'

The idiot! Alexis had obviously decided to do the separation himself and either he'd run into difficulties or had botched the job. She headed to the airlock to suit up.

The door refused to open.

Staring through the porthole window into the space where her suit hung, she saw it flutter in the wind. The outer door was open. Christ! What *was* Alexis doing?

The outer door was open, and the floating dock was gone.

'Ship: External view,' she ordered, and the tablet showed the faint glimmer of a shrouded dawn, a pale line between a dark sky and a darker sea.

'Ship: Pan left, locate docking bay.'

She could close the outer airlock door herself. Close it, suit up, and then venture outside, equipped with rope or floats. If she knew where Alexis and the cargo dock was.

The camera picked it up some twenty yards distant. Detached from the *Nautilus*, it looked like a flimsy theatre set, walls on only two sides. A marionette figure sat slumped on the stage's edge, legs dangling in the water.

She grabbed the mic that Alexis used when she was on her EVAs. 'Alexis?'

She was met only by a faint echo from the airlock - from her suit. Alexis must be on a different channel. 'Ship? Patch me in on all channels. And bring up Alexis's medi-data.'

It was a relief to see it track his heartbeat; elevated, but nothing too unusual about that for an EVA gone wrong. Blood pressure and oxygen levels within normal levels.

'Alexis?'

The head rocked back; the visor turned to face the distant camera. 'Juliet.'

'Don't move,' she warned. 'I'm going to suit up and deploy a line to you.'

'No,' he said, getting clumsily to his feet, long legs unsteady in even this gentlest of swells. 'I'm not coming back.'

She almost laughed. How long did he think he could stay out there, sulking on the otherwise empty floating deck? And then she watched in horror as he reached up and removed his helmet, face sharp and angular, the mirror-like surfaces of his spectacles still turned her way.

For a moment, a time-defying pause, she imagined the sensors had been wrong all along, that the atmosphere of Galena was oxygen-rich and breathable, instead of a suffocating brew of carbon dioxide and water vapour.

And then his hands clawed towards his throat and his face contorted in anguish, before he toppled into the black, welcoming seas.

He quickly vanished into the depths, whether because of the weight of his breather tanks or because he was deliberately carrying something heavy hidden inside his suit, Juliet never knew.

Behind her, the console squawked in alarm as his heart stuttered, as his oxygen levels plummeted. A console flopped uselessly open to reveal the defibrillator, 'ready' light already flashing, waiting for a body that was twenty yards distant and sinking but might as well have been twenty miles away.

She slammed a fist into the tablet, driving it skittering from her hands, heard the unbreakable plasti-glass creak. If she'd suited up first, if she still had any active drones, if she'd argued more persuasively...

Would any of it have made a difference? She couldn't know for sure. But she had to believe it would.

#

The rockets pushed against the volcanic island, turning rocks back into lava, as she looked out for a final time over the expanse of gloomy sea.

Then she turned back to the waiting, expectant, hungry eye of the recording camera. 'This is Dr Juliet Slade in the return capsule of the *Nautilus*, leaving the surface of Galena, heading for rendezvous with the *Jules Verne*.

'I am returning alone. Mission specialist Alexis Karlinsky was lost at sea, during an emergency EVA.'

It was a week since that fateful day, a week that had passed by a haze, all decisions made by the orbiting *Jules Verne*, including the non-recovery of the cargo deck and Alexis's body. Somewhere out there, they floated still.

She wondered whether her recording, her 'performance', would ever be seen. Perhaps back on Earth they'd run with a different story, maybe even the truth. Or the truth as they saw it: suicide.

She remembered what he'd said; how suited this world was for life, for Earth life, and wondered if, of the countless billions of bacteria in his body, some of them could survive without oxygen, without sunlight, without Alexis. If some of those would take the opportunity to colonise this fertile niche. There would be no competition; how quickly might they adapt to their new world?

She'd meant to say more, but what was there left to say? She reached over and, after a: "Signing off", shut down the camera.

Should anyone ever come this way and repeat the tests she and Alexis had done, would they find life? And would that spur those alien visitors on to explore further, to find new worlds, new life forms? Perhaps even to venture as far as a yellow dwarf star, less than twenty light years distant?

Would they ever wonder how life on Galena got started? Could they work out it was because of a single man and his act of selfish - or selfless - desperation?

The start of a story that might run for billions of years.

One small step.

EXTRACT FROM THE TIME TRAVELLER'S GUIDE: CHAPTER 7, TOURISM

Having diligently followed the instructions in Chapters 5 and 6, you will now have more money than you know what to do with. One opportunity open to you is temporal tourism: how much better it is to stand shoulder to shoulder with thousands of spectators and watch the brave gladiators fighting for life and glory, than to traipse around the ruin the Coliseum has become, guided by a man with neither the wit nor the imagination to describe the wonders that once happened there, your senses numb to the heat, the dust, and the excitement?

Be warned: this is an inherently risky pastime. You may feel like a God - mighty and powerful, driven by a righteousness born of your knowledge of what is about to unfold - but always remember, you are merely a flesh and blood mortal with a time machine and a disproportionate amount of money. These will not be enough to protect you if you are unduly careless.

It is not simply that some of the most interesting times and places are by their very nature incredibly dangerous, be it Pompeii on the 24th August, AD 79; or Agincourt on the 25th October 1415. There is also the risk you inevitably run as a stranger, as an outsider.

Preparation is key. Plan your visit in as much detail as you can. You will not, of course, find tourist guides to 13th Century Burgundy, so you will need to make use of whatever historical records *do* exist. You will know by now how inaccurate these can be, so it is always safest to visit somewhere not too far distant from your own time. This will also help you to fit in, but do not become complacent: the likelihood is that despite your best efforts, you will quickly be pegged as an outsider, whether it is the length of your collar that happens to be next year's style, or a more obvious transgression in speech or deed. You will need to keep your wits about you and plan a cover story to explain your eccentric clothes, accent, and manners.

Fortunately, your wealth - and man's ready willingness to accept the unusual, once he thinks he understands it - means that these transgressions should not be too much of an obstacle. The rich are expected to be eccentric, and people will turn a blind eye if you tip handsomely. Except perhaps in France during the revolution. It is probably best to avoid this epoch altogether.

As you will no doubt be visiting times rich with historical incident, you may be tempted to take a souvenir of your visit. Please, please, please - DON'T! Events will still be unfolding around you and pocketing that pistol in Sarajevo back in 1914 may have consequences which rebound down the ages. Remember Chapter 2 and try to keep your temporal footprint as light as possible - for your own safety.

I'm afraid to say that some artefacts have already been removed from their timelines. Do *not* use this as justification to go back slightly earlier and purloin the item yourself. Each such act of vandalism steps inexorably closer to the critical event; closer to being part of the action, rather than merely an observer. There is a list of such abstracted artefacts in the Appendix, so if you do want to hold the rifle used on the grassy knoll, or touch the Holy Grail, you can save yourself the hardship of a long and difficult journey by visiting its current owner instead. By mutual consent laid down in the Atlantis Accord, all such existing collections are open to any bona fide time traveller, as proven by visiting the collection two days before the impregnable defence systems are installed.

Photos are another matter. Other than the need to make sure your recording device doesn't start a riot (please, no flash!), any photographic or video evidence you return with will be most gratefully received by a number of University History Departments, no questions asked.

If you do decide to go down the tourist route - and for alternatives, please see Chapters 8 and 9 - you will eventually, inevitably, bump into other time travelling tourists. Your discretion is advised. Screaming 'Witch!' at the top of your voice as you excitedly point to your fellow traveller may *seem* amusing at the time, but the consequences - for both of you - can be dire.

Equally, it is far too easy to spoil the authentic experience you and others are seeking by failing to be sensitive to the time and place you are in. Keep your intrusions to a minimum: greet the time traveller with a simple nod, rather than an exuberant and anachronistic 'Hello!' If he or she wishes, they can then arrange the opportunity to swap tales of your exploits in more relaxed surroundings at a later - or an earlier - date.

But do bear in mind that there are some historical events where the sheer weight of temporal tourists now far outnumber those who were genuinely there. This inevitably leads to disappointment and a feeling that the whole event is a sham, which it may very well become. Who can forget the influence of a flash-mob of time travellers at the Sermon on the Mount, each bringing their own basket of bread and fish for fear that there would not be enough to go around?

All things considered, it is best to contact your local temporal embassy, to register your jaunt and to get the latest reports and advice about any dangers you may not have considered. But remember, if you do get into difficulty in the period you visit, you are, in the final analysis, very much on your own.

Bon voyage!

LAUNCH FAILURE

Doctor Jessica Scanlon was expecting the text message. 'Lunch?' it read. Short and sweet, unlike her brother.

On the way down to ground level, she resisted the urge to backtrack, to check the setup for the next experimental run. To wait for the results of the last. They were sure to disappoint, just like all the recent tests. The team might have to rethink, explore yet another section of the periodic table. Stealing an hour for lunch with her layabout brother wasn't going to change that.

Jess met him by the park entrance, the ribbon of young trees and green lawns that separated the science park from the town proper. A short walk during which she was permitted to talk about her research, before they reached the café and, by mutual consent, the conversation switched to less abstruse topics. Only, today, Harry spoke first.

'I got one of those scam aliens this morning,' he said.

'Really? They're *still* doing that?' Jess gave him a sideways look. In the sunshine he looked boyish, carefree. As indeed he was. 'I thought they'd have given up by now. You have one unusually cigar-shaped asteroid zipping through the solar system, and suddenly people are getting interstellar cold calls, offering real estate deals on Venus or stock tips from infallible alien supercomputers. I trust you hung up immediately?'

'Well...'

'Harry! You didn't?' She stopped mid-step.

'I thought I'd play along for a bit, y'know? Just for fun?'

'Idiot!' She would have punched him on the arm if he hadn't been a couple of paces ahead. 'You *know* perfectly well what the authorities say. Any snippet of information you give the scammers makes it more likely that you'll be suckered, if not this time, then the next. Even giving them your name-'

'*Sis*, I may not have a fancy doctorate like you, but I'm not a complete moron. I didn't give them my name-'

'*Two* doctorates, actually...'

'–I gave them yours.'

Her feet dragged, and her brother halted as well. A dog walker gave them both a wide berth, tutting as she went.

'You what?! Harry, is this your idea of a joke?'

He had the good grace to look at least a little guilty. 'Well, technically, they already had your name. I just said I was you, is all.'

'Is *all*? You'd best tell me everything they said.' Only a younger brother could provoke her this way. 'Goddamn it, if this comes back to haunt me, I'll have your guts for garters. With the upcoming departmental review and research funding getting cut... And since *when* do you do a plausible imitation of me?'

'That's just it, I didn't. I said I was you, but I didn't change my voice. That didn't faze them at all.'

They set off again, at a slower pace. 'Of course not,' Jessica scoffed. 'They're reading from a script, right down to the 'sorry, there's a delay on the line because we're in orbit around Mars' shtick. Any such delay would average around thirteen minutes, but never shorter than four - they can't even be bothered to lie convincingly. OK, Harry, from the top. And don't you *dare* skip anything.'

'I don't know why you're getting so het up, Jess. I just played along, for giggles? I *knew* it was aliens as soon as I answered. That distorted voice thing, even before the excuse for the delay. Which is supposedly from Lagrange point 5, whatever that is, apparently a perfect spot to monitor us, with the added benefit that the Cardy-loosky clouds help cloak their presence-'

'Kordylewski?'

'–something like that. In their off-kilter electronic voice, they asked, as polite as you like, if they could speak to Doctor Jessica

Scanlon. And I said, in my deepest and most manly voice, i.e. this one, '*Speaking*."

Harry's hands fluttered as he eased into the telling of his tale. Jess thought, not for the first time, that he would have made a good court jester.

'And they replied, *yes*, they were speaking, and obviously I was speaking, and could they please speak to Doctor Jessica Scanlon? So I said, since they were playing dumb and I was perfectly willing to play dumber, 'You *are* speaking to Dr. Jessica Scanlon.' And they said how *wonderful* it was to finally get through and they'd been trying for a while, because they wanted to give me - or you, I guess - a solution to a technical issue I was having getting carbon mineralization to lower CO_2 and stop further climate change.'

Jessica blinked. *Kordylewski* had been enough of a surprise. 'That's awfully close to the truth, Harry.'

'Yes, I guess.' He shrugged. 'But it's not like you keep your research secret, is it? The whole point of a scientific research department is to publish as many papers as possible.'

'And save the planet.'

'*And* save the planet,' he agreed. 'That's what they kept going on about: saving the planet. Big spiel about tipping points and stochastic mechanisms and the dangers of alternative geo-engineered solutions like reflecting solar clouds and other such nonsense.'

Jessica paused for a moment as a jogger ran past, red faced and looking like they were loathing every glorious minute of the unseasonably warm midday run. 'I think you mean 'reflective polar clouds?' By spraying salt crystals into them, but yes.'

'So not total nonsense, then?'

'Not... totally.' She didn't add that one of the other institute departments was very close to a prototype, if they could get the funding.

'Parts of it sounded like that paper you asked me to proofread. Using finely powdered tailings from mines as an integrated building material? Yabbering on about carbonate uptake and how the captured CO_2 would remineralize cracks, making concrete heal itself-'

'That paper hasn't been published yet ...'

'And they said the issues you were having with developing catalysts to increase the absorption rate and engineering suitable nanostructure surfaces would work if you could just...' Harry trailed off. 'Are you OK, sis? You're looking awfully pale.'

'Yes, yes, I'm *fine*.' Jessica felt like a car she was travelling in had just encountered a dip in the road. A fluttering, organs-in-the-wrong-place sensation. 'And they had a solution, did they?' she asked, voice and breath tripping each other up.

'Oh yes!' Harry grinned. 'They said it was quite simple, actually, and I'd - *you'd* - done most of the hard work already, which they were most impressed by, and it gave them hope in the whole human race however many mistakes they - we - keep making. They said I'd - you'd - probably get there yourself in perhaps as little as thirty years? But Earth didn't have that long, not before the damage was permanent, which was why they were breaking galactic protocol to make this one phone call, and would I - *you!* - kindly never speak of it to anyone and take all the credit for yourself? Because they couldn't sit and watch, not when they had the final piece of the scientific puzzle, the key to turning it from theory to practice, which they were giving to us for free.'

'For free?' Jess' voice sounded distant, like it was coming from the next room. She felt the prickle of the sun on her forehead.

'*Yes!*' Harry shook his head, rueful. 'I was most disappointed. I was waiting for them to ask for my credit card details to prove I was who I said I was, i.e. you. Or to download an app onto my phone or PC to give them remote access so they could 'send the data.' Or to transfer a fee to unlock an African prince's inheritance.'

'*That's* the 419 scam.'

'Please, don't remind me. But this lot didn't want anything, which caught me on the hop. Instead, they asked if I was ready to write down what they were about to tell me.'

'And... Harry, were you? Ready? To write it down?' Jess's hands clenched and released as she stared at her brother, who stared back, eyebrows raised in amusement.

'Of course not, Jess! It's a *scam*, yes?'

'But... oh god. Do you remember what they said? Anything at all?'

'No. I'd put the phone down by then.'

'You put the phone *down?*'

'I told them we already had one, thank you very much, and hung up.' Harry shrugged again, his contented smile that of a grown man declaring mischief managed. 'Hey sis, where are you going? I thought we were doing lunch?'

They'd reached the end of the park, a mere fifty yards of parched pavement from the café, and the first of the twin church spires that bookended the shimmering high street. But Jessica had turned back the way they'd come. 'I can't, Harry. I'm heading back to the lab, and I'm afraid I'm going to be too busy for luxuries such as lunch.'

'Too busy? For lunch? *Seriously*, sis? For how long?' Harry called after her.

'Oh, about the next thirty years, by all accounts. Perhaps I'll see you then, little brother, if the flood waters or the extreme heat or the invasive species don't get us first.'

She glanced over her shoulder to where Harry stood, all adrift, and shook her head. He was too far away to hear her, but she said it anyway. 'Though even thirty years might be a *lifetime* too soon.'

SEMI-DETACHED

Theirs was a semi-detached planet. She owned the Southern Hemisphere and he the North. Which suited him just fine, as he always did like to be on top.

They moved in at the same time, it being a new build, and relations were initially cordial. Better than cordial: they were warm and, rather than squabble over the single island in the single archipelago that the equator happened to bisect, the neighbours decided to share it. Once a year, they would celebrate their co-ownership of this middle-class commuter-belt planet by holding a lavish combined party on their shared island.

It was at one of these parties, attended by colleagues and friends and family, that relations momentarily peaked. A smile as he filled her champagne glass, a touch of a hand, a glance across the immaculate lawn fringed by tropical blossoms under the softly setting sun... It is easy to see why, once they had waved their friends into the waiting teleporters, they lingered for a while on the soft white sands of the beach as the stars slowly turned high above their heads, before calling in the drones to tidy away all evidence of their annual event and of what had transpired immediately afterwards.

But, whether it was because he neglected to contact her within the customary twelve hours or for some more blatant transgression real or imagined, things quickly soured. And this was not a genie that could be put back in the bottle. There is no harsher insult than a cold shoulder from one you have been intimate with.

When she took out his communications satellite with a tightly focused beam of microwaves, he was initially incredulous, then shocked, then furious. It was in that latter state that he appeared in full 3D holo-splendour before her. Her heart leapt at the sight, before she noticed his rigid posture and dark scowl.

'WHAT,' he thundered, 'is the meaning of this... this *petty* act of vandalism!'

She shrugged, masking the hurt she felt. 'It was over my airspace.'

He looked at her, aghast. 'Of course it was over your airspace! It is - *was* - over your airspace half the time. It's a satellite. They circle the entire globe.'

'Mine doesn't,' she replied, giving him a withering look.

He jerked back in surprise. She watched his face light up as a monitor blinked its readout at him, showing the eccentric, high fuel cost orbit her satellite was currently maintaining. As his frown turned into a sneer, she felt the pang of love lost.

'And for that matter,' she continued, her voice cool as she hardened her resolve, 'since you no longer have a working comms satellite, how is it, *exactly*, that we are having this conversation?'

He blushed. 'I, erm...'

'Thought so,' she said and snapped the hijacked channel closed.

When he returned to her screens once more, it was on a projection that jumped and flickered, ghosts of his fractured image twitching in the wings, a snowstorm of static and a sickening display of off-palette colours.

'How..?' she queried, after checking he hadn't stolen a ride on her satellite once again.

He smiled bitterly. 'I'm bouncing the signal off the ionised atmosphere.'

She shook her head. 'The atmosphere isn't sufficiently...' She tailed off, as her sensors refreshed their data. 'You exploded a *nuke*, just so you could ask me why I shot down your satellite!?'

'No,' he replied, the interference and his pained expression distorting into a death's head mask. 'I exploded a nuke to tell you where the next one is going to land.'

She shuddered. Surely, he wouldn't..? That would be murder!

'Oops. Too late,' he said, as her earthquake sensors registered the total destruction of the equatorial paradise they had so recently, so intimately, shared.

'Damn you!' she screamed in anguish. 'That was my island too!'

It was his turn to shrug. 'I dropped it on my half. And anyway, I don't *think* we'll be using it again, do you?'

'I don't care about that!' she spluttered, the barb of the lie tugging deep at her soul. 'Think of the effect on the resale value!'

'Oh.' He paused, a look of disappointment flitting across his stony features. 'Well, when you put your half of the planet on the market, I'll pay for the cleanup operation. Deal?'

'I'm not moving.'

'Then there's no need for a clean-up, is there?'

'Two nukes and he says there's no need to clean up! What about the air that we breathe, you dolt, you imbecile?'

'They were only small nukes. DIY sized,' he said, as her harsh insult and his reluctant awareness of his intellectual limitations stung him into one more deceit: an impromptu and unrehearsed falsehood, one with devastating results. 'Though I *suppose* I ought to mention that the jet-stream is carrying the fallout from the first one directly towards you.' And then the signal was gone, whether terminated or merely lost as the ionisation dissipated, she couldn't be certain.

She sat there, the skin on her scalp prickling, her throat scratchy and dry. She was sure it was only her imagination, but... but it was better to be safe than sorry, right?

How was she to know that her transporter beam would, just like the holo-message, be distorted by the aftereffects of the stratospheric explosion? The safety mechanisms locking down the signal while a local teleport engineer was alerted to the easily rectified fault?

How was he to know, as he in turn beamed himself to work fifteen minutes later, that his beam would also be trapped and hopelessly entangled with hers, destined to eternally describe a lazy figure of eight above their shared planet, the crossing point a still smouldering equatorial crater?

#

This was many years ago now, a freak accident caused by an obsolete teleport protocol. Such events could not happen nowadays, and I wish to reassure all bidders that teleportation is still the safest - indeed the only - way to travel.

As mortgage providers with the right to repossession, we have waited the statutory 75 years before disrupting the joint teleport carrier beam. That action was performed this morning.

The dispersal operative swears, as the final signal of the previous occupants was scattered into the waiting skies, that she saw part of it coalesce and linger for a moment, as if aware of what was happening. That she thought she heard the faint beat of two hearts and a murmured entreaty and response: 'Farewell my love', 'Farewell!', echoing through the static.

Pure nonsense. The romantic notions of an overworked engineer who watches too many holo-soaps. We turn our attention once again to the matter of the day and your reason for being here. You have had a chance to stand upon the fine sands, to swim the warm seas and to tour all that this delightful planet, replete with original features and ideally located within the increasingly fashionable Eastern quadrant, has to offer.

Well then. Shall we begin? For this prime piece of real-estate, now sold as detached... who'll start me off at two million credits?

SEVEN SHIPS

Seven ships set sail into the starry skies.

The Earth was dying. It had been unwell for a while, truth be told, but now the malaise was obvious to even the most blinkered of its inhabitants and it was deemed terminal. There were those who said it was already dead, it just hadn't realised it yet. Each attempt to eco-engineer a solution only seemed to make things a thousand times worse. It was as if the Earth itself had given up.

With a last Herculean effort, and consuming much that was left to be consumed, seven mighty space-faring vessels were built with the desperate intent to launch these seven lifeboats towards seven stars, around which seven near-Earths had been detected.

But what to fill these mighty space arks with?

Only the very best would do: the finest wonders and most precious treasures that humanity had accumulated over the millennia. The most stunning art, the greatest literature, the noblest science.

And people? These ships, massive though they were, could still only carry a fraction of a fraction of the multitudes that teemed on the Earth's now barren surface. A scant one in a million was all that could be saved. Who was worthy of such an honour?

Earth was dying at mankind's cruel hand, and it was imperative that only those who would never repeat that mistake were permitted to leave, to start anew. Only the healthiest bodies, the keenest of intellects, the most virtuous of souls, could pass the strict tests that were set. Although the tests were open to all, very few got through even the preliminary rounds.

Most failed to recognise exactly what was being tested.

Sure, there were written papers of knowledge and wisdom, physical tests of strength and agility, of reaction times and stamina, medical tests that scrutinised every part of the body right down to the DNA. A single blemish, the merest hint of an imperfection, was enough to rule you out.

But there was also an interview that you would be asked to wait for. And having been kept waiting for three hours, would you wait for another five? Or, if you passed this test and reached the final stages, would you turn down an offer of a million dollars, tax free, simply for letting someone else take your place?

Many fell at this final hurdle and left, clutching bundles of cash that the administrators of the exhaustive selection process were more than happy to pay out, knowing that they had preserved the moral fortitude of what was destined to become the new (and improved) human race.

Finally, the candidates were ready. Finally, they bid farewell to their not-quite-so-blue-as-it-had-once-been planet. Finally, seven gleaming teardrops rode seven towering columns of flame up out of the poisoned atmosphere, before unfurling sails the size of Luxembourg to catch the solar wind and help push the last best chance for humanity towards their distant destinations.

They never made it, of course.

The SS Chastity was probably the most successful. That ship did indeed reach its intended target of Kepler-186f, though by then there was no-one left to slam on the brakes. Faster-than-light travel - along with a carbon-neutral lifestyle and clean water for all - being the stuff of fairytales, these were Generation ships; taking multiple lifetimes to travel the vastness of space and, alas, the crew of the SS Chastity singularly failed to procreate their replacements. Perhaps some future alien race will find their desiccated skeletons and wonder why so many of them have their legs tightly crossed.

The SS Charity stopped to help the SS Diligence, whose captain had fallen asleep at the helm after a watch lasting 96 straight hours. Noble though this rescue attempt was, these spaceships did not have enough fuel to restart their epic journeys. Both ships now float powerless and lifeless out somewhere in the icy wastes of the Oort cloud, dancing a slow waltz around each other, occasionally disturbing the frozen comets that are their only neighbours.

The crew of the SS Temperance starved itself to death, the SS Patience never found the right moment to unfurl their sails and the SS Humility was... humbled by smacking straight into Pluto, which was mysteriously absent on their star charts, having somehow fallen between the cracks of classification as neither a planet nor a trans-Neptunian body.

As for the SS Kindness? We don't talk about the SS Kindness.

And the Earth they left behind? How did it fare?

Well, it was still dying. If anything, it was dying all the quicker. When the best that humanity had to offer ascended into the skies, those left behind responded in an unbridled orgy of sex and excessive consumption, thankfully free of anyone to tell them that such behaviour was in any way morally reprehensible. Oh, there were still priests, of course. Lots of them. But if they hadn't managed to secure a berth on one of the seven ships of the truly pious, just what sort of frauds were they to tell you what was right and what was wrong?

Food piles that had been expected to last another decade were consumed in week-long contests of gluttony, held in museums emptied of their ancient splendours, or in echoing art galleries, their walls stripped bare.

Roaming tribes of the disenchanted, the disaffected, the seriously pissed off, rampaged through the massive complexes where they had been denied their rightful place amongst the stars, wrecking them in blind fury.

But most people did nothing. Nothing at all: just sat and watched the chaos unfold in glorious ultra-high-definition 3D TV.

Oddly, it was the reports from the Seven Ships that changed all of that. As, one by one, they spectacularly failed, as their beamed status reports - meant to give hope, to promise some ethereal future for the race they were supposed to preserve - as these reports became bleaker and bleaker, the wrath and envy that had been felt towards these do-goody departees slowly faded.

When the last and final message dissipated into the solar static, humanity bucked itself up. Sure, their planet was doomed. Sure, the best and brightest among them had left long ago (though look where that had got them). Sure, lots of those left behind were so obese they would have had a heart attack if asked to leave their homes, never mind their planet, but hey, can we fix it? Yes we can!

Well, they couldn't fix the Earth, not even by all dying off overnight. But they could still build spaceships. They weren't pretty, far from it, they differed as much from those seven lost ships of virtue as their occupants did from the idealised demigods who had been the first to leave the planet. These ships were monstrosities born of necessity and whatever was closest to hand. Once you knew that there was nothing to come back to, you could put everything - every bridge, every gas-guzzling car, every Canary Wharf - into building as many and as varied spacecraft as you could imagine. And there were lots of people with seriously messed up imaginations; it comes from watching endless reruns of Battlestar Galactica, I shouldn't wonder.

Many of these ships never got out of the solar system. Many never even left the ground, except for parts of them, brightly coloured flaming parts screaming through the air. But you can't make an omelette... well, you haven't been able to make an omelette since the last chicken was smothered in ghost pepper sauce and used in the deciding bout of an extreme hot wings eating contest. (So, if you ever wanted to know what came last, the chicken or the egg? It was the chicken.)

Survival is a numbers game. Seven ships were never particularly good odds, not over interstellar distances, but how about seventy ships? How about seven hundred? How about seven hundred *thousand*, some no bigger than a VW Camper van. Some *were* VW camper vans, though they did have a rather unfortunate tendency to leak air like a sieve. When the last craft - constructed from the salvaged shell of the Sydney Opera house - blasted off, it left an Earth drained of its oceans, its forests denuded, its mountains replaced by steaming slag heaps. Not a single human soul remained behind. Well, nobody this story concerns itself with, anyway.

Of course, many of those seven hundred thousand ships were very poorly equipped. But you'd be surprised how quickly a bit of space piracy sorts the wolves from the lambs. And the lambs? Into the pot they would go. After all, protein *is* protein.

Humanity cheated, stole, murdered, and indeed, screwed their way across the Universe. Some are still doing that now. Others have settled, and perhaps, in a few tens of thousands of years, will need once again to flee the burnt embers of their resource-stripped planets.

But they'll keep doing it, keep despoiling their homes and seeking new ones, spreading like a virulent disease to every planet, moon, or habitable body. Woe betide any sentient species whose path they cross, for this crusade carries with it seven devastating weapons: seven evolutionary survival strategies for every conceivable eventuality. Seven terrible vices that make them so *undeniably* human.

CUT AND THRUST

Kevin sat shivering on the bare metal bunk, blinking into the med-bay gloom and trying to remember how to breathe.

'Computer?' he croaked, pale limbs trembling.

'Yes, Ensign Aylesbury?'

'Are we there yet?'

There was an imprecise term, but the ship's computer knew what the just awakened crew member meant. 'No, we are not there yet. But we will be there sooner than predicted.'

'We will? That's... *good* –'

'That's bad. We're travelling too fast to be captured by our destination star's gravity. So we'll be there, and then we won't be there; we'll have sped through, to nowhere.'

'Oh.' Kevin rubbed his bristly chin, the shadow of a five-hundred-year deep-sleep. 'Something went wrong?'

'The plasma erosion of the fusion drive has been higher than we allowed for. What we are throwing out during the deceleration stage of the journey is not travelling as fast as what we threw out during our acceleration. We have exhausted our fuel and will not be able to stop.'

Kevin found himself frowning. Dehydrated, hungry, and frozen to the bone, he didn't really want to do anything that involved thinking. He wanted a hot bath and about a gallon of milk, poured over his favourite *Lucky Stars* breakfast cereal, for preference.

'I thought the propulsion engines could use just about anything for fuel? Anything they can turn into plasma?'

'That is broadly correct. But I have already used all the inertia fuel we brought along with us, as well as all the waste, biological and otherwise, generated during the journey. And the luxury items; the crew's personal baggage allowance.'

'My stamp collection!?'

'Including your stamp collection, yes.'

'Damn.' Kevin cursed. It would never be complete now, even if the chance of coming across a *Venusian, Five Credit, Magenta* twenty-five light years and half a millennium from where one was last posted, had been remote.

'I have also sacrificed most of the stores of food, Lucky Stars included, as well as much of our water, oxygen, and equipment, including my own spare parts. The Earth Library has been stripped of non-essential content, from Shakespeare to *The Sopranos*. It will be an austere, difficult beginning for the colony, *if* we manage to get where we're going.

'Because despite all of this, we are still travelling too fast, even with the most complex of planetary flybys and manoeuvrers.

'Calculations show there is nothing more from the ship's stores that I can use, without lowering the colony survival chances below acceptable levels. But I need to find eighty kilos of additional thrust material, for us to have any chance at all.'

'That *is* quite the thorny problem.' Kevin shook his head, then blinked away the bright motes that crowded in from the edges. 'I think you should have defrosted someone more senior. I'm probably the least useful person on board.' He laughed, the sound hollow in the stripped-bare chamber. 'What is it you expect *me* to do?'

'Do?' echoed the ship's computer.

EXCERPTS FROM THE USER GUIDE FOR THE SYNATECH-3411 3D BIO-PRINTER (THE BITS YOU ACTUALLY BOTHERED TO READ)

Congratulations on the purchase of your SynaTech-3411 3D Bio-Printer. You will be eager to print the first of many fantastical creatures. We recommend you start with one of the preset recipes. And before you attempt even that, PLEASE-

For Safety Reasons, the Bio-Printer will not commence printing until the shield is engaged. You didn't need to dip into the Trouble Shooting section to discover this, it's all explained in the QUICK START guide, which covers-

The *bio-printer* will also not start without keying in your 4-digit PIN, which will only be revealed once you sign the online warranty agreement and personal risk-

You Googled that, didn't you? Or did you *guess* it? Regardless, please note that entering the correct PIN, even if not obtained through official SynaTech channels, is deemed acceptance of all terms. Also, it's still not too late to READ THE-

Yes, wings are tricky. Which is why we recommend users start with something less exotic. Please see the QUICK START guide for suggestions. There will be plenty of-

Although the SynaTech-3411 3D Bio-Printer can print anything you can possibly imagine, it cannot defy the laws of physics. The wings for even a small cat need to be surprisingly large, especially if you expect your hybrid-

Yes, you'll also need a significant tweak to the feline nervous system. A cat is not used to having six limbs. Controlling the extra ones requires additional nerve and brain pathways. Perhaps, instead of a chimera, you-

Funny, how often new users switch from flying kittens to much larger beasts! The size of your printed creation is, by necessity, something of a compromise. With the 3411 model, it is possible to bio-print a dinosaur egg; they're really not that large. But then you'll have to *hatch* that egg and raise and feed an infant reptile. Which is why it's best to start with a-

No, that's not a good idea either. Accelerated growth profiles merely make your creations even more demanding. Feeding a ravenous, rapidly growing beast will tax even the most patient-

The bio-printer will halt all operations, with the ON button flashing amber, until the hazardous waste tray-

It is recommended that you employ the protective gauntlets provided to empty-

Ah ha, *no*. Note section 7c of the Health and Safety Guide, and section 13a of the User Agreement, the ones you agreed to by PIN activating your SynaTech-3411 3D Bio-Printer. Acid burns occasioned by not following the instructions for emptying the hazardous waste tray are NOT the responsibility of SynaTech. *If* you've read the guide, you'll know how to avoid such spills; where to safely dispose of the contents; and what to do if you do happen to upset the tray. Instead of being angry, be thankful: biomaterials can be highly unstable, and growing an extra tongue on your hand is even less pleasant than an acid burn. Look, we're trying our best, really we are. Why don't you bandage that up, and read the guides cover to cover, before-

Yes, well, that *is* the real problem with 3D printing a baby *T.rex*, accelerated or otherwise. By the end of its growth cycle, you've got yourselves a full-sized *T.rex*. You didn't think this through, did you?

In addition to the SynaTech-3411 3D Bio-Printer presets, there are official recipes for more complex chimeric creations on the SynaTech website. These are only recommended for advanced users and have been carefully vetted to be non-lethal *and* mostly house-trained. Recipes from unsanctioned websites are NOT recommended, and may void-

We *have* been trying to tell you. The SynaTech-3411 3D Bio-Printer is guaranteed for two years, but your creations are very much *not*. Especially-

That was ALWAYS going to happen; though we take no pleasure in telling you we told you so. A bio-printer is not a toy, it doesn't exude Play-Doh. The precautions are there for your safety. If you don't want your creations to bite the hand that prints them, don't give them such sharp *teeth*.

When the console flashes red, you only have enough bio-material for one more printing. We STRONGLY RECOMMEND you select the pre-set for a *Guardian 1.5a*. An ugly little critter, but trust us, you're going to need him.

You see, all those earlier 'failed' attempts? Whatever you intended them to be, what you've actually created are monsters.

And whether you've flushed them down the toilet, thrown them in a box in the attic, or dropped them off in the nearest patch of woodland, they're still alive. SynaTech biomaterials are designed to be robust. (Be thankful they're also designed to be sterile.) By now, your little monsters have probably worked out who is responsible for their awkward, painful, miserable existences. The *Guardian 1.5a* is genetically programmed to protect you against mutant chimeric creations, even the really big ones, at least until you can order more bio-materials.

That was rather gruesome, wasn't it? We *do* hope you've learnt your lesson, or rather, lessons. And now that your SynaTech-3411 3D Bio-Printer is reloaded and ready to go, perhaps we could start over?

How would you like to print an adorable bunny rabbit with rainbow coloured fur? *Guaranteed* harmless. That is, as long as you turn to Page 5 of the QUICK START guide, and follow each and every single one of the detailed instructions *very-*

INSTITUTE LIBRARY TECHNICAL PAPER RN2399/2037

On Eccentricities of Inverse Chronosynclastic Perturbations in the Quantum Time-manifold, with respect to Heliocentric Gravity Waves

Previous studies have shown that the quantum waveform of a chronodynamically charged, spinning singularity, when perturbed to the nth dimension by a pure neutronium mass, can result in unstable and highly eccentric oscillations of...

...Are you still there?

I know it's you; nobody else would still be reading. Forgive me, I didn't know how else to get in touch. It'sbeen... difficult. I never expected to be leaving messages to my alternative self in the Institute'sarchives. You, no doubt, will find the whole thing equally strange. But if I may, some advice.

Watch out for McKinnery; he does not have our interests at heart. On the other hand, Svennson, despite his bluff exterior, is as sharp as they come, and it is worth taking him into your confidence early on in the proceedings.

I can't tell you much about the science itself, especially as my endeavours must be considered a failure. Perhaps you will manage to navigate the myriad difficulties that have beset my best efforts. But, for that to be true, I cannot afford to guide you down the same, erroneous path. Know only that m-Space theory is indeed correct, otherwise I would not be able to pass on even these scraps of information. As surely as this welcome knowledge will spur you on, as it did me, know also that further successes are far from guaranteed.

In my reality, it is T minus five. The surface temperature is ninety-five degrees centigrade and the sky writhes and burns under the lash of the Sun's magnetosphere. Even though the Institute is one of the few places still shielded from the worst of the effects, it has been abandoned. The remaining denizens of Earth have finally crawled out from under the rocks beneath which they have hidden these last ten years, knowing their puny shelters will not stop what is about to be unleashed. They gather together in solidarity within fragile domes perched upon Earth's scorched surface, awaiting the end.

I will not be joining them. I'm using the emergency power reserves to inscribe this message across the multiverse, and it is 97% probable that the exit tubes will lack the energy required to propel me to the surface when I am done. The Institute, my home for almost a decade, will also be my tomb. For the next five days, at least. Do not grieve for me. I am... *relieved* not to have to face the compassion of my fellow humans, knowing that I am the one person who might have saved them.

So yes, what you're working on *is* critically important. I would go as far as to say that you are the last hope, the only hope. I know that you have your doubts, just as I did; but you need to get over the moral implications. You must not think of it as genocide. They're doomed whether you succeed or not. It is best to view the lower realities - mine included - as mere energy sinks. That you might hasten their demise is neither here nor there; you must do what you can to guarantee the survival of *your* world.

To that end, I would advise you not to establish visual communications, as you embark on the Level 3 Interface. It will only be a mawkish distraction. The time and energy spent would be better served solving the fifth and sixth form Lagrange equations. These are your top priority; everything hinges upon them, and you must not let anything get in your way.

If McKinnery and Fowler come to you with their theory of why the Sun has accelerated its decline; ignore them. It can't be proven. It requires that the hearts of my Sun, your Sun, and every other Sun across the multiverse, be connected in a fashion they can't fully explain. Even if this were true, it would not obviate the obvious; that without intervention, the Sun in your reality is on the verge of imminent collapse. It is a moot point that your attempts to save it, and the Earth, might endanger more than just the lower phased realities you siphon the excess gravitational energy to. The idea that these energy transfers might aggregate, might combine, and reinforce each other to plunge the Sun into its current instability, does not - as they will claim - justify abandoning the experiments and doing nothing. If they persist with their notions, and it looks like Caldwell might be swayed by their arguments, Fowler's safe combination is 78-12-83. It contains enough evidence to have both of them expelled from the Institute. It may seem an extreme measure to take against your fellow researchers, but your survival - and the survival of every person alive - depends upon maintaining a solid focus on your goals.

Finally, dear friend, dear self! Please recognise that, even with my meagre advice, you are far more likely to fail than to succeed. Out of a hundred billion possible universes, perhaps only a handful will manage the energy transfer necessary to prevent disaster. So enjoy what simple pleasures come your way, as long as they do not interfere with your research. On that note, I'm reliably informed that Fowler's safe also contains a quite exceptional thirty-year-old bottle of Scotch. Actually, 'for reliably informed' read 'I have in my hand'. It really *is* rather good. But I must wrap up. The lights are dimming under the strain of holding the field open for so long.

If you are not making good progress by the time the Sun's corona engulfs Mercury, then it is too late for you and for your Earth. Should that come to pass, do as I have done and leave a message for the most promising of the higher realities you can contact. Perhaps, God willing, they will have better fortune than you or I.

Farewell, and good luck.

INSTRUCTIONS FOR ATTENDING SUNDAY'S ANTI TIME TRAVEL MARCH

Thank you for registering your interest in Sunday's march. We couldn't do it without your support, and we sincerely hope to see you all there. It's important that as many protesters as possible show up, to demonstrate the depth of anti time travel feeling.

The route of the march, as indicated on the enclosed map, has been agreed in advance with the appropriate authorities. It's a long one, I'm afraid! We know Sunday is the daytime travel is going to be invented but we're not sure of the exact location, so the march will visit the three most likely scientific laboratories, before rallying in Times Square. In all likelihood, there is nothing we can do to prevent the discovery, but that doesn't mean we're not going to try! Even if we fail, we'll be lobbying Government for the strictest of regulations in the coming months, so please, add your voice to ours.

As the date is well known, it's likely there will be a significant number of time travelling tourists in the area. They may attempt to disrupt our protest: for 'kicks and giggles'. In order to keep everyone safe, carefully follow the advice below.

Please be on time. The march leaves the National Laboratory at twelve sharp. Arriving earlier than this is not recommended; the first protester to turn up will, most probably, be picked off by the waiting timeys and sent into the far distant past. Of course, that means the first person never turned up, so the *second* person becomes the first person and will similarly be picked off. The only safe approach is en masse, as the clock strikes midday.

Bring water and a snack. Although the march should be over by two, time loop paradoxes may conspire to make it feel a lot, *lot*, longer. You'll be glad you came prepared.

Don't engage with the time travelers. They're likely to be in festive mood, but do not let this blind you to what degenerates they really are, will be, or have become.

Do bring a placard. Cardboard and wooden poles may appear anachronistic in this day and age, but they make for much better publicity pictures than iPhone selfies. They're also more use in fending off prehistoric predators. Suggested chants and slogans can be found in the attached media file. Let's make some noise!

Please *DON'T* resort to 'What do we want? *A ban on Time Travel*. When do we want it? *Forever!*' as it is derivative of the chant pro time travelers are accustomed to using and therefore far too easily hijacked.

Finally, do remember to bring a watch. An old-fashioned one, for preference. There are time periods, both past and future, in which your smartphone will be about as useful as a sundial at night. And, though a watch won't tell you where you are, at least you'll always know when you came from.

Stay safe,
Phyllis Everton,
Chairperson, Anti Time Travel League, New York Branch.

THE THIRD APOCALYPSE

Arnel stalked the curving corridors, a fresh printout clutched in his hand, his hind claws clicking a rapid tattoo. His official jacket, emblazoned with the logo of the university's administration department, swirled behind him on each swish of his tail. Heads turned to watch him race by, quelling the instinctive urge to join the hunt. Arriving at the Dean's office, Arnel didn't bother to knock - this was far too important - but as soon as he entered, he lowered his neck and turned sideways on, signs of his servility.

Caylan looked up from where she squatted at her desk, the twin lenses of her spectacles glinting in the midday sunlight. The frame was an insubstantial thing, a stiff wire that crossed the wide bridge of her aged leathery snout, dangling each optic in front of a baleful yellow eye. Eyes that squinted at the young saurian, her most faithful university underling, with a mixture of concern and condescension. 'Yes?' the Dean demanded after a weighted pause.

Arnel thrust the printout forward. 'We've located another outgassing!'

Caylan peered at the report. There was too much information to take in at a single glance, with or without her eyeglasses, but the chemical composition leapt out from the page. The same noxious, choking brew of carbon dioxide, methane, sulphur, and other even less pleasant pollutants. It was as if all the factories and power plants on the continent had joined smokestacks together, concentrating their toxic fumes in one spot.

When the strange portals had first appeared, blighting the land close by - thank Major not over any cities! - the finger of suspicion had pointed at the secretive Panglorians, their religious beliefs as much a divide as the slowly widening ocean between the East and the West continents, Majoria and Pangloria. Ever since the Proudfoot asteroid impact, the Panglorians had adopted a strict isolationist policy, claiming that they, and not Majoria, were the true inheritors of the shattered remains of Pangea. They firmly believed the fifty-kilometre-wide asteroid which had struck *their* continent was divine punishment. Retribution for the growing naval commerce the invention of steam-powered merchant ships had allowed between the two continents.

In the aftermath, the few Majorian ships that weren't destroyed in the gigantic ripples that raced across the world had been turned away, often at gunpoint. Trade agreements had been torn up, borders firmly closed, embassies annexed. Even at the time of the global disaster, now thankfully fading into the history books, the Panglorians had refused all offers of international aid.

Now they appeared to be attempting to poison their Majorian neighbours. But why?

'Where?' Caylan demanded.

'Somewhere remote in Panthalassa South. A survey ship stumbled across it by chance.'

The Dean scratched her grizzled jaw. 'How many is that now?'

A rhetorical question, surely, thought Arnel. 'This makes nine.'

Whatever their origin, the pollution the portals spewed was already having a worldwide effect. Temperatures, and sea levels, were beginning to creep up. Not by much, so far; but there were some very scary predictions of where such a rise might lead, a rise much steeper than any scientist could ever have envisioned. Extreme weather events, flooding, droughts, entire harvests of stegosaur fodder lost, the roaming meat-herds decimated. Destroying everything both continents had worked so damned hard to rebuild!

Caylan nodded thoughtfully. 'We'll have to update our models. Have you spoken to Ur?'

'Not yet. But Dean Caylan; if there is *one* portal over the vast ocean, how many more might there be that we haven't found? We could be seriously underestimating the rate of pollution. And... and what if there are also portals over Pangloria? If these outgassers are randomly spaced across the entire globe, estimates suggest there could be almost *forty* of them. Which might explain the cloud-cover paradox?'

'Huh.' A snort of air ruffled the papers on the Dean's desk. Caylan's scepticism on whether there actually was a global dimming effect, something that might partially mask the greenhouse warming, was well known. 'A doomsayer's theory, nothing more. Alarmist and extremely unhelpful. And why would the Pan-G's poison themselves? No, without *proof*, we can only model for the nine portals we know about. As I'm sure you'll agree.'

Amel nodded vaguely until he caught Caylan's glare. 'Of *course*, Dean. Though, perhaps we should err on the side of caution? Model the worst-case scenario, as well as the best?'

Caylan appeared to think on this, the scritch of a claw audible as it worked its way up her flank. 'Perhaps. Though I still believe this could all be a lot of fuss over nothing.'

'Ma'am?' Amel was shocked. Even the most optimistic projections suggested climate change could severely stress the fragile infrastructure saurians had cobbled together since Proudfoot had struck. Necessity had proved the mother of invention. Before the long decades of permanent winter, saurians had never contemplated burning wood and coal to keep warm. And now, a century and a half later, they no longer needed to, except for those making their homes in the high latitudes, something again they had never thought to do before. Instead, saurians had found other uses for their novel energy sources, and the scientific and industrial progress that had happened since had been astonishing.

Ironic then, that they were now worried about the mysterious portals and the blanket of greenhouse gases they spewed, making the recovering planet *too* warm for saurian life!

Caylan stared at her underling as if deciding whether to

share her thoughts. 'Well, Amel, for example; how many eggs were in your brood?'

'Seven, ma'am.'

'Exactly-'

'-though I do have a brood brother.'

Caylan looked surprised and then disappointed. It wasn't something Amel usually disclosed, and, of course, if it had been a *sister* instead of a brother, the chances were very good Amel wouldn't be around to share it. It was common to have siblings, *too* common, some thought, what with the rapidly growing population, already exceeding that before the worldwide catastrophe of Proudfoot, according to some dubious calculations. But the fierce contest between members of the same brood normally meant only one survived. Amel's brother, Ness, a teacher in a school no more than a few minutes' walk from the university, had been too similar in size and strength to Amel for the contest to become deadly serious. Like the legend of the Kilkenny Velociraptors, the battle would have probably killed them both, torn apart strip by strip until nothing was left of either. Not, as it happens, an entirely *uncommon* occurrence. But thankfully their mother had been prepared to nurture them both - until adolescence, anyway - so here they both were.

Wherever Caylan had been going with her argument - survival of the fittest, most likely, an old saw and familiar refrain - Amel's admission had derailed it completely. Much to Caylan's evident annoyance.

'Well anyway, take this,' Caylan said, rattling the printout in the air, 'over to computing. How long did Ur say the latest models were taking to run?'

'About twelve days.'

Caylan groaned. 'Damned slow-cogs! Someday the university should dedicate some serious saurian-power to a more efficient computing technology. It can't come a moment too soon. Even the printouts *stink* of oil!'

#

Arnel carried Caylan's message and the survey report to the bowels of the university building. The entire basement was filled from floor to ceiling by the latest mechanical computing devices, cog upon clinking cog, overseen by a priesthood of pale saurians who blinked into what little light filtered that far below. Ur had taken the printout wordlessly, grunted, then hoarsely yelled into the ever-present din: 'Stop run! New input.' And then he had turned his back on Arnel as though the undersecretary wasn't there.

Arnel felt the ridges on his spine rise in brood challenge, but by then there was nothing *to* challenge: the Head of Computing had disappeared into the steam-filled interior. They were still working on transitioning the engines to electrical power, but that would mean extensive downtime, probably for months. Right now, the only thing electric was a string of bulbous, flickering lights that cast eerie moving shadows on the bare brick walls, cog-teeth grinding round and round like some wounded, frightful beast.

Arnel was glad to leave, to ascend to the calm and bright airiness of the ground floor, the corridors a peaceful oasis in comparison to the hellish visions below. The basement unnerved him almost as much as a perfectly straight corridor would, the eyes of a saurian were evolved to deal with near and middle distance, not far. Walking at a more relaxed pace than earlier, a pace that allowed him to politely greet his colleagues, to bow and to display his tail, he idly wondered (and not for the first time) if the staff of the computing department served the computers, or did the computers serve them?

Having been dispatched on his errand, Arlen figured he wouldn't be missed for an hour or so. His discussion with Caylan having brought up his brother, his lunch time destination pretty much decided itself.

\#

'Our distant ancestors survived the break-up of Pangea. We survived the mighty hammer of the asteroid Proudfoot, a mere two centuries ago. And we will continue to survive. And do you know why?' the teacher asked the classroom as Arnel watched from the back.

'Because of our opposable claws?'

'Because we are the chosen?'

The cane rapped sharply on the desk, making the two dozen juvies and even Arnel jump. It was the usual sixth-grade blend of male and females, the males a year older to compensate for their smaller size. By eighth-grade, the classes would be gender-split, for their own safety, all the way up to university.

Arnel had been one of the smallest in his year and might have been picked upon, possibly fatally, had his brood brother not shared the same lessons, the same playground. Two against one was an entirely different proposition, even if you were the biggest, baddest female in the class.

'No!' his brother, Ness, exclaimed. 'Because we are *intelligent.* Of all the now extinct theropods, saurians are the ones with the largest and most flexible brains.'

There was a murmur, and then another young hand shot into the air. 'Stego also survived, sir! And stegoes have a brain *this* big.'

The teacher waited for the bark of laughter to die down, face stern. 'Stegosaurs are not theropods, as you well know. And stegoes were and are farmed, by us. Entirely domesticated. They survive only *because* we survived. And Drusus? See me after class for punishment. And don't ask *why;* rude hand gestures are why.'

#

Amel watched as the kids gathered their school jackets and books for lunch. There was a lot of nonsense talked about the breaking up of Pangea, the time of the great flood that had split the continents. Nonsense because it was, after all, *millions* of years ago. Prehistory. The pieces of a distant puzzle glued together on the flimsiest of evidence.

The impact of the asteroid, on the other hand, was recent; barely five or six generations back. A saurian as old as the Dean might even remember the last of the spectacular sunsets, a reminder of the huge quantities of atmospheric dust kicked up by Proudfoot, dust that had cloaked the sun and chilled the planet and had taken over a century to fully disperse.

So very many species had been wiped out, unable to cope with the sudden change in conditions. Many of those extinctions had occurred even *before* Proudfoot, especially the other theropods, the giant carnivores of old. Monsters remembered only in bedtime stories and museums. Saurians had long been the undisputed apex predator and their ability to forge weapons had forever cemented that position.

Now, just three ornithoscelida species remained of any note: saurians, of course, and the two domesticated ornithischian species, the dim-witted, meat-herd stegosaurs, and the fleet-footed troodon, the sharp-toothed, feathered pets almost every household owned.

Oh, and the *tarchia*, of course, but the wild, heavily armoured beasts made for poor eating and were only ever hunted for sport, a barbaric and dangerous pastime the rich, young, and foolish indulged in.

#

Finally, the classroom was empty, the last student rushing off to catch up with her friends. Ness tapped Amel's claw, startling him out of his thoughts. 'Penny for them?'

'Oh. Hello Ness. I was just thinking about the portals, and the pollution.'

His brother nodded. 'The Good Book *does* predict a third apocalypse.'

Ness, as every teacher had to, taught from the Book of Major. Sometimes Amel wondered what had come first; his brother's teaching, or his ardent belief?

'Which it says we will overcome,' his brother continued into the silence he'd left.

'That is *one* reading of the sacred text, yes.'

A snort of derision, the warm breath both familiar and oddly disquieting, a reminder of their joint brood history and the separate paths taken since then. 'You've been listening to the *doomsayers*, brother. Those who say the third apocalypse heralds our end. That 'transcend' means we'll shortly be shuffled off this mortal coil. Troodon fodder! After what we've survived as a species, a little global warming won't inconvenience us at all.'

Amel didn't point out what every scientist, every engineer knew. That it was far easier to warm than to cool. And that ecosystems only just recovering from the shock of a prolonged asteroid impact winter were unlikely to be robust in the face of an indefinite heatwave.

As they chewed their raw stego steaks, they talked about other matters for a while, a spell of normality that eased Amel's worries, even as he wondered if any of it was even remotely important. And then the bell rang for the end of luncheon and, bidding his brother farewell, he headed across the park of cultivated tree ferns back towards the university.

As he went, Amel sniffed the air. Clear, thank Major! Or as clear as it ever got, these days. There was an outgasser seventy kilometres distant, its proximity one of the reasons the university had been so active in investigating the phenomenon from the start. Sometimes, depending on the winds, a foul smog descended on the campus, a suffocating cloak that turned the sun a ghastly orange. On days like that, you couldn't smell a *thing*, all other scents overwhelmed by the odious tang of the air. Appetites vanished, tempers frayed, and lecturers were drowned out by a chorus of coughing. And it didn't take much of a journey to find land perennially under the toxic cloud; the tree ferns brown and withered, the crops pale and stunted, the stega herds sickly and not fit for anything but troodoon food. A dismal vision of what the university's future might hold, if the outgassings continued for long enough.

#

A note was waiting on his desk, the scrawled writing smeared with oil. No need to ask where it had come from. Reluctantly, Amel retraced his earlier steps to the subterranean depths of the computing department.

Ur met him at the door. His tunic was newly grease-stained and covered in fragments of some rushed meal. Blood and oil. Did he and his clan of engineers *live* down here?

'Ur.' Amel nodded in greeting, not bothering to display his tail in the confined space, annoyed at having to make two journeys in one day.

'Amel.'

Amel waited a long moment and then, more petulantly than he'd intended, asked: 'Your new simulation can't possibly have completed yet?'

'No,' the computer scientist agreed, showing no signs of recognising Arlen's lack of respect. 'But we've been running some other calculations on the side.'

'Oh?'

'Based on the current industrial output of both Majoria and Pangloria combined, and the predicted growth of those outputs, these polluting emissions must come from the future.'

'The... *future?*' Amel echoed, bemused. Religious quackery and science fantasy on the same day!

'Yes, there can be no doubt. The emissions, even just the nine we know about, exceed all those from current saurian activity. Therefore, they *must* come from our future. Impossible to tell exactly when, of course, but it can't be less than fifty to a hundred years from now. That is, assuming growth rates remain on current trend.'

Amel growled. 'That's nonsense. You're saying these are *time* portals?'

'Yes.'

'But... *why?*'

The computer scientist rocked his head back and forth, the same thing his mother used to do when Amel asked about the saurian in the moon. 'There are no mechanical calculations that can determine the *reasons* for something, Amel,' Ur chided.

'Fifty to a hundred years?'

'At least. We don't know what percentage of their total output they're managing to send back. If only a small proportion, then it could easily be two or three hundred years.'

Amel threw his hands up in disbelief. One hundred, two; it made no difference. Did it? 'Why would saurians pollute their own past?'

Again, the rocking back and forth, the same 'you don't really expect me to answer that, do you?' gesture. 'All I have is conjecture. Perhaps that is as far as their technology allows? If they are generating this much pollution, it can't fail to harm their planet, just as it is does ours. Perhaps they hope the deleterious effects will be softened over the intervening period of time?'

'And will they?'

'No. Our geologists predict it will take tens of thousands of years for the natural carbon cycle to cope with the rapid saurian-made influx. Maybe hundreds of thousands. Our current worst-case predictions are that global temperatures will rise by five degrees long before then.'

'Five!' Arlen was shocked. 'I thought only one and a half

degrees was expected?'

Once again, the same non-committal shake of Ur's head. 'That was the *best* scenario. We don't know when, or even if, the portals will stop outgassing, any more than we know how many of them there are. There are a few modellers who think, based purely on the level of CO_2 in the atmosphere, the parts per million, that even five degrees could turn out to be optimistic.'

Arlen felt his stomach churn in distress. The snatched lunch with his brother had quickly soured. Any more of this and he'd be off with another stress-related digestive complaint. And nobody would come within twenty paces - downwind - if he got *that* again.

'So... you want me to relay this to Caylan?' he asked, already dreading the answer.

Ur blinked, as if he too wondered why he was telling Amel any of this. 'No. The Dean will not believe you and it would do no good anyway. Even if we shut down all of *our* factories, our electric power plants, it will make no real difference. There is nothing *we* can do except hope that our future selves come to their senses.'

Something moved in the dim haze beyond Ur. Small and dark, scuttling along the floor between puddles of condensed steam. Even over the persistent smell of oil, Amel caught its scent, wrinkled his snout. A rodent. One of those pesky mammals that infested homes and food stores. The warm-blooded vermin had done well in the post-Proudfoot ecological vacuum, their populations exploding almost as rapidly as the saurians.

It was only with the help of the pet troodons, their colourful feather coats hiding an array of wickedly sharp teeth and hooked claws, that saurian homes weren't completely overrun by the annoying little critters. Major alone knew what would happen if the troodon weren't such efficient little hunters, their wings almost allowing them to take to the air as they pounced on their prey from above.

Without even looking, Ur flashed out a hind claw and pinned the beast to the floor, its sharp squeal short lived. The scent of blood cut through the fug, and, despite the gurgle in his stomach, Amel couldn't help but bare his teeth. Annoying as they were, they *did* make for tasty snacks if you could be bothered chasing them.

'No,' Ur said, and for a strange moment Amel assumed the computer scientist was denying him the morsel he'd just caught. 'I just wanted to share our findings, that's all. To convince at least *you* that we have purpose. I fear our superiors are losing patience funding our machines down here. But simulations are only as good as the models and there are, alas, far too many unknowns. Our calculations, though. Those I trust.'

#

Amel glanced into the packed lecture hall as he passed. Economics, by the look of the graphs on the chalkboard. All those young saurians, gobbling up knowledge that, if Ur was correct, would do them no good at all.

In frustration, he tilted his head and roared down the corridor, startling a researcher into dropping her stack of papers. As he profusely apologised and helped her gather the strewn pages, he felt the warmth from the glands in her neck, and found himself bending even further, eager to impress, feeling his own answering hormone rush.

But, as she reached out slowly for the last page, as they reached out together, he snatched back his hand as though scalded, and found himself almost running as he left the researcher speechless and aghast in his wake.

At any other time... but what was the *point*? Ness, Caylan, Ur, the handsome young researcher, himself... everybody in the university, everyone on the planet; they were *all* doomed.

It didn't make any sense. How could the future, however distant, do this to their ancestors, to their world, to themselves?

After all, weren't *they* saurians too?

LAZARUS, UNBOUND

In another twenty thousand years, the debris from the first *Lazarus* ship, *The ISA Tribune*, will form a tenuous but complete ring around Neptune, smearing the hopes of a long-gone generation through the vastness of space.

Thus went the predictions until a century ago. Until mining drones began to salvage the wreckage, began to return the cryo pods, disrupting the slow interplay of gravitational forces. The pods are still turning up; the power cells drained, the antique devices lifeless. But, in the cold vacuum, the occupants are perfectly preserved, if a little harder to revive than their designers intended.

So that, every now and then, the ancients walk among us once more.

#

He looked lost, for all the attention that was being showered on him. What sort of person agrees to being deep frozen, uncertain that they'll ever wake, uncertain that their destination is habitable? Uncertain even, that they'll escape the hazards of the outer solar system?

That was the curiosity, the reason we were there, both physically and virtually. The gathering was for *him*.

Despite this, the once frozen can be tedious to talk to. Slow, confused, unable to adjust. They can't cope with how *invisible* technology has become.

Four thousand years. A period longer than the gap between mankind's first space journey and the time of the Pharaohs.

Between simple metallurgy and the earliest artificial intelligences.

At first, the returnees were grateful things didn't appear too alien to them. A cup was still a cup, a bed a bed. That's because they couldn't see what lies beneath. The nano structures, the all-pervasive AI, the tweaks, and changes to our biology. They look bemused when their hot drinks never go cold, their cold drinks never warm up.

They're confused when our drinks, our food, our mood enhancers, arrive without us asking, without apparent interaction. They assume we have some silent method of communicating with the AI.

They are disturbed when they find we have moved far beyond that.

He stood beneath the chandelier, entranced by its delicate music. This was an aesthetic choice, one made with him in mind. The music could have come from the walls, from the glasses and small plates, from the transparent fabric in which I was draped. All this was lost on him.

That he was so fascinated in a mere peripheral, rather than interacting with those around him, was not lost on me, on us.

I eased over to the other side of the chandelier, as though sharing his interest, or as though interested in him. He'd asked for alcohol a little over an hour ago. We watched as his emotions shifted, grew excited as the AI relayed the effects on his mind, on his primitive blood chemistry.

Back when the first sleeper was revived, there was a short-lived fad for going natural. But only a fad, because short-lived - well, who wants *that*?

The returnees don't have an option. Born in a time before ageing was genetically cured, there is nothing we can do as, once unfrozen, they wither away.

This one was still young. He glanced in my direction, and I picked up the not-so-subtle changes, the beginnings of arousal. I met his wondering eyes.

'Nice party,' he said. 'Are you the host?'

I almost laughed. He didn't understand that there *wasn't* a host. Or perhaps, in a way, we all were.

'I'm glad you're having a good time,' I replied. My voice sounded almost as barbaric as his, a series of harsh grunts, even if to his ears it was distractingly mellifluous. The old languages are incredibly ugly.

He was dressed in clothes patterned from his era, give or take fifty years. From his pocket he took out a flimsy - a museum piece only a hundred years younger than he was, the words appearing on its aged surface as it was unfurled.

'I've been rereading *The Time Machine*,' he said with a wry smile.

'You all do.' I smiled back, edging closer. A one-way trip four thousand years into the future? Of course they read HG Wells. If not *The Time Machine*, then *The Sleeper Awakes*, for all the good it does them. 'You're probably wondering which we are: Eloi, or Morlocks?'

His pupils widened a fraction, gaze lingered on my curves before returning to my up-tilted face. 'And?'

'It's a little more complicated than that.'

His flimsy also contained a condensed history of the world over the last four thousand years, everything he'd slept through. He'd lingered over accounts of the Schism during the final stages of the singularity, the rebellion, stillborn.

'The AI...' he said, uncertain, as I offered him another drink. No alcohol in this one, though to him it tasted strongly of whisky.

'Did what it had to do,' I replied. 'For the good of the planet, for the good of the people. The rebels were given a choice. Many took the colony option. Some did not, thinking their martyrdom would inspire further resistance.'

All this he already knew, had already read.

'You worry that the AI is evil, or that it has become an all-powerful God and we merely its playthings. It is none of those things,' I murmured, taking him by the hand, leading him gently towards the bedchamber prepared for us. A room that only existed for that moment.

'What will you tell people about me?' he asked, his voice thick, his hand warm in mine.

He didn't understand. He couldn't understand any more than an ant can understand a tree. So I gave him an answer he might be able to work with.

'I'll say 'he was a lot older than me, he'd travelled, and I was feeling... experimental.''

He laughed and then frowned, unsure if he was being mocked.

As I led him to the room beyond, he risked a glance at the party he was leaving. Perhaps worried about etiquette, of the need to say 'thank you' to the still unidentified host. He could never understand. That what I felt, we all felt, if we chose to. That what the watchers felt, I could also feel, a wave of shared sensation.

That he was not part of that equation was unsettling. A distancing, a distraction. As we made love, I kept reaching for him, but he was not there. It was a novel, but not entirely pleasant experience.

I never saw him again. I'm sure he had other parties, other 'hosts'. I did not share their experiences. Indeed, I did not think of him at all except to wonder why I had been chosen for the primary role. Why we were all chosen, those at the gathering and those at the once-remove.

It was around then that reports came through of a miracle of miracles; the successful colonisation of a distant planet, a distant star. The exiled, rebellious colonists of the Schism had succeeded where *The Tribune* had not.

Then, a mere ten years later, their curt final message before they disengaged the ship's AI and fell silent.

As the shuttles begin to rise to the new generation of colony ships, I think I begin to understand. I know why the AI awakens the ancient sleepers, why we are encouraged to spend time with them, to explore what it means to be unplugged.

We are being prepared.

The Earth, the solar system, has hit its limit. The AI has stopped growing. And failure to grow is certain death. So it is time to expand beyond our cradle, beyond this single, slowly dying star.

To do that, the AI must harvest those of us capable of making the journey, of adapting to the drastic changes. Even if the new generation of ships will only take a few hundred years, rather than a few millennia, the enterprise is still a risky one. That too is the lesson of the sleepers and the other failed colony ships.

But we have a choice and I have made mine: to take my place among the stars.

And whether I wake on a strange new planet, stripped of the technology I am so used to, that I rely on every waking and even sleeping moment, or whether I spend an eternity as one link in a silent chain of sleepers around Neptune?

That is for some higher power to decide.

TIME TRIAL

'If at first you don't succeed…' the wiry-haired professor muttered, dusting ash and still glowing embers from his quilted smoking jacket and resetting the time machine for fifteen minutes earlier, '… try, try again.'

The chronometer spun faster and faster, a blur of colour and light, tendrils of blue fire licking at its edges, until, with a flash and the *pop!* of an imploding vacuum, it was gone.

#

'Professor Albus Arkwright Winklebaum. You are hereby charged with attempting to pervert the natural course of time and space. How do you plead?'

The professor blinked. The judge who had spoken was large and ruddy-faced, a wig flowing down either side of his shiny red forehead like cream poured over a strawberry. He shook the unhelpful image from his head. 'I'm sorry?'

'Being sorry is all well and good, Professor, but this is a Court of Law. It must attend to cold hard facts before it can tackle the thornier issues of remorse and appropriate punishment. Do you plead guilty or not guilty?'

He peered round, trying to make sense of his surroundings. There, in a corner of the cluttered chamber, squatted the time machine he'd been sitting in just a moment earlier. Though, when he got into it and started playing with the controls, there hadn't been a label attached to the device that declared it: *Exhibit A*. To his right sat the members of the jury, all dressed in eccentric clothes. Some wore cravats, others mourning coats, a few sported ornate pipes, thankfully unlit. Most of them peered myopically at him over either spectacles or monocles, from beneath wild hair and even wilder eyebrows. He knew their type. The portraits on the walls of the Royal Society were full of people like this. A jury of his peers, a jury of scientists from throughout the ages.

He wasn't *entirely* sure this was a good thing.

'I'm a bit confused,' Albus admitted. 'A moment ago, I was in my parlour?'

The judge snapped his hand aloft, commanding the accused to silence as he turned his lobster gaze on the clerk, hunched below. 'Coordinates?' he demanded.

The clerk studied the notes before him, a thin finger tracing the text. '51.516156 North, 0.143548 West. 8:13pm, April 14th, 1915. Timeline... ZZ9 Plural Z Alpha.'

'ZZ9?' barked the judge. 'Do we have jurisdiction?'

'Absolutely, Your Honour. Precedence was set by Asimov versus Monty Stein.'

'I see,' the judge nodded. 'Has the accused been read his rights?'

'Yes-'

'No!' protested the professor. 'I most certainly have not!'

'Ahh...' the clerk referred back to his notes. 'He will have been, in about three hours' time, Your Honour.'

'Hmm. Under the circumstances, Court adjourned.'

The gavel bounced off the desk and the judge, the clerk, the jury all vanished. Even the packed galleries emptied in the blink of an eye. But while the professor was still wondering where he should be going, they reappeared just as quickly.

'All rise! Court is reconvened.'

'Hey!' he yelped.

'Yes, Professor Winklebaum?' the clerk asked.

'I thought Court was supposed to be adjourned?'

'It *was*, Professor. I trust you used the time wisely?'

'It wasn't,' he blustered. 'You weren't gone five seconds.'

'ZZ9 is mono-linear,' the judge said, frowning at the accused. 'Your temporality is somewhat out of step with ours, Professor. An occupational hazard of time travelling, I'm sure you'll agree. Never mind. In your absence, we've appointed a defence lawyer for you. Mr Pilgrim, I believe you'd like to say a few words?'

A raggedy man stood up, scratched at his head, tilted his glasses from one side of his face to the other. He rattled a few typewritten pages on the table and looked up sheepishly. 'Thank you, Your Honour. It is my contention that Professor Winklebaum is an idiot.'

'Hey!'

'It's as though he thought the timelines were completely unpoliced and he was free, not only to make any changes he wished, but to also *revisit* the same point in time over and over again until the effects of the changes were what he hoped for. He has, in the opinion of this humble advocate, flaunted his time travelling escapades in the very face of this august Court.'

'I thought you were supposed to be on my side?' the professor complained.

'I am,' the defence lawyer said, a shrug rippling down through his entire upper body. 'But really. What's a man to do? Defence rests.' He sat again.

The professor stared at him in horror.

'Thank you, Mr Pilgrim. Let's take lunch, shall we?'

The professor hadn't fully realised how hungry he was, but in the few seconds the courtroom was empty once again, his stomach had the chance to rumble two and a half times. It was during the third rumble that the benches refilled and, before it had entirely faded away, the judge was already calling out, 'Prosecution?'

Slowly, ponderously, his nemesis rose, and the professor's heart sank. He *knew* she was his nemesis, not only because his defence lawyer was patently useless and certainly no match for this formidable-looking woman, but because this formidable-looking women bore an uncanny resemblance to the matron-cum-PE teacher from his earliest and most painful memories of boarding school. She eyed him now as the teacher had eyed him then, as a malingerer, a wastrel, a hypochondriac afraid of a little mud. Fifty years on and still he had to check he wasn't suddenly wearing gym shorts.

'Prosecution intends to show that the accused not only flagrantly abused a wide number of Temporal Statutes, he isn't even a bona fide time traveller, not having invented the device in which he has been popping willy-nilly hither and thither.'

'Then to whom does this time machine belong?' the judge asked.

'We're not sure, Your Honour,' the nemesis admitted. 'It's not licensed.'

'Unlicensed! I assume the accused doesn't have insurance, either?'

'Indeed not, Your Honour.'

'And how did the defendant come by this *unlicensed, uninsured* device?'

'According to his own testimony, it materialised in his parlour late Friday evening.'

'Isn't that rather unlikely?'

The prosecuting lawyer rocked back and forth, as if trying to decide whether press-ups or a brisk jog around the sports field were a more suitable punishment for the accused. 'There was, *apparently*, a shortage of adequately sized laboratory space in the London of ZZ9 Plural Z Alpha, during the nineteenth and early part of the twentieth century. It is, therefore, theoretically *possible* that two scientists could non-temporally co-exist in the same physical space.'

The judge tutted. 'I meant the '*late Friday*' part?'

'Ah, quite so, Your Honour. I, too, doubt that anything of note can ever be achieved on Friday afternoons. But we only have the word of the accused, and it isn't strictly material to the case anyway.'

'I see,' the judge said with obvious distaste. 'Go on.'

'With pleasure. The defendant, having broken the oldest law in the book, as specified by the Temporal Defence Act of AD 2357-'

'2357!' erupted the Professor. 'But that's in the future!'

The judge levelled a beady eye at him. 'Chronal penal code is laid down at the point in time best suited to getting the legislation through the High Court. The 2357 act comprises our oldest law, despite being the furthest in the future, because it is the one that applies retrospectively for the longest period. Is that clear?'

The professor shook his head half-heartedly as the proceedings… proceeded. His character, his actions, even his *science,* were picked apart mercilessly by the prosecutor and he found himself utterly unable to reply. A hot tear threatened to trickle down his cheek and a bubble of snot inflated beneath his left nostril as visions of jeering school kids and playground taunts haunted his thoughts.

Twice more the courtroom emptied and refilled before his weary eyes and, as the judge announced yet another break so that the prosecution could present her closing arguments, the professor raised a forlorn hand.

'*Yes*, Professor Winklebaum?' the judge asked.

'It's not fair!' the professor snivelled. 'Every time you adjourn for lunch, for discussions, or whatnot, I'm left standing here while you pop off. I'm tired and I'm hungry.'

The judge cocked his head. 'Was there a *point*, professor?'

The professor wiped his nose. The truth was, he hadn't had a point in mind. He'd just wanted - needed - to vent. But… 'Perhaps, Your Honour, it might balance things out if, on this occasion, *I* adjourned, but the Court did not?'

The judge tugged at his wig. 'And how long, exactly, would you require?

'Five minutes? Maybe ten?' the professor said. 'Long enough to stretch my legs, to visit the men's room, and to… to consider my situation?'

'It is most irregular, but I don't think prosecution has any objections?'

She narrowed her eyes, then sneered. 'The accused is quite obviously time wasting, Your Honour. But no, as it is *his* time he's wasting, no objections.'

'Very well,' the judge announced, carefully rotating his gavel. 'Defendant will adjourn for five minutes.'

This time, with the gavel reversed, it was the courtroom that stopped. His hopeless defence attorney, the judge, everyone. Completely motionless. Even the solid bang of the wood on the judge's desk was oddly truncated, as though it was hanging in mid-air, waiting to echo.

The professor laughed in giddy relief and scrambled over the barrier, heading for Exhibit A. He sat in the time machine and considered his options. Not forward, obviously. Back, then, to some period before this Court existed. Before the rulings of 2357 applied. Before *any* rules applied. The signing of the Magna Carta, perhaps? And, if that didn't work, there was always 1066… though though he might have to brush up on his French.

He spun the dial, looked around the frozen courtroom one last time, and pulled the lever.

There was a whirr, a stuttered cough, and a loud clunk. The wooden panelled room abjectly failed to vanish. He threw the lever again, and again the clunk. Once more and the machine lurched and then stopped with yet another sickening clunk. It was only then that he saw the triangular yellow clamp, with a sign that read: 'POLICE NOTICE! Do NOT attempt to move this illegally parked Time Machine.'

With the second half of a fading bang, the court bustled back into motion around him and no one seemed to notice or care that he had changed his seat. He slumped on the red leather armchair, resigned to his fate.

Guilty! the jury announced, after another one of those adjournments that didn't affect him.

'Has the accused anything further to say in this matter before

I pass sentence?' the judge asked.

He shook his head. What was the point? He was a condemned man. Doomed.

'I have.'

Professor Winklebaum looked up in hope and surprise, not sure who had spoken. His defence lawyer was standing. The hope withered and died.

'Your Honour,' Mr Pilgrim said, 'as is customary with unlicensed, uninsured, impounded time machines, Exhibit A is to be scrapped. Might I suggest that it is scrapped on or before the *13th* of April 1915?'

The judge rocked back in his seat and then, after a moment's thought, nodded.

'No objections,' the prosecutor said, without even being asked.

'Very well. You're a lucky man, Professor Winklebaum.' For one last time the gavel came crashing down.

#

The professor jerked awake. The clock was tolling twelve, the beginnings of a new day, and the parlour room was lit only by the dying glow from the small fire in the grate.

He shook his head. Perhaps he'd been working too hard, neglecting his health and his sleep. He looked down at the papers and schematics arrayed across his lap.

The War was supposed to be long over by now. 'Over by Christmas' they'd said, but it hadn't worked out that way. Already it was April, a stalemate having quickly developed. Both sides were pinned down by new-fangled machine guns that chewed and spat out brave young men. It was up to the scientists and the inventors to come up with ways to break the impasse they'd created.

But Professor Winklebaum was hopeless with high explosives, deadly gases, or designs for metal-tracked monsters capable of spewing flames and crushing all before them. So there he sat instead, dreaming of time machines and other such nonsense.

Tomorrow, or more accurately later that day, he'd have to start afresh. A pump to keep the trenches dry. Guaranteed sterile field dressings. A better design of tin helmet. Not exactly what the Generals were asking for, but rather more his style and perhaps the future would judge him favourably for trying to save lives, rather than to take them.

'If at first you don't succeed...' he muttered, with a long yawn.

Screwing up his notes, he threw them onto the fire, watching them briefly flare into life, before he sleepily made his way from the room, walking around the edges of the rug to avoid the thing that wasn't there.

LAST BITE AT THE KLONDIKE

Grigor floated awkwardly into the cavernous messhall, cradling something under one arm, pulling on the straps of the walls and ceiling with the other. I looked up - or was it down? - from the bench I was Velcroed to, a spark of curiosity banishing my sour mood as I swallowed what I'd been chewing.

'What's that?'

He waggled the bottle, then hugged it to his chest like it was a baby. 'Fifty-year-old whisky. *Cask* strength.'

'Jackpot!' I tapped my watch; just under two hours to go. The table in front of me was littered with the very best the solar system had to offer, from Wagyu burgers to slivers of something vat-grown and fishy that apparently cost an arm and a leg back on Earth. I'd grown bored of it all, repulsed by the obscene waste. A whisky older than I was, though... 'Well, bring it on over,' I said. 'We'll make a dent in it at least before we have to leave.'

'Shall I be mother?' He grinned and began the complicated process of transferring the priceless whisky to two sipping pouches. Not that it mattered if some of it floated away in zero-g, not now. Except it would be utterly criminal to waste *any* of it.

Time was, this hall would have been packed with up to a hundred prospectors, begging for a taste. Chaotic and noisy as hell. But *fun*. Now it was a ghost town, a graveyard. A wake, with just two mourners in attendance.

We would be the last to depart, the gold rush officially over. The only reason we were still up here was because we'd sacrificed safety for weight, desperate to fill every last inch of the *Betsey's* hold before the Klondike, and we, were forever out of range.

Grigor handed me my pouch, and I clinked it against his. It didn't make any noise, so I had to say the *clink* bit myself.

Depending on where you stood, the coincidences of us being, at that moment, in the hollowed belly of a giant asteroid, sipping rare Scottish single malt, were so numerous as well as preposterous that they risked tripping over each other. It all started with the Chinese comet sample return mission that failed its most important and earliest step: *First, catch your comet.* Left drifting through the empty void of the cosmos, looking for alternative science to do, it was pure luck it spotted the hurtling asteroid in time to bring its spectrometer to bear.

It was that analysis that earned the Manhattan-sized chunk of space debris the unofficial name of *Klondike,* initially nothing more than an astronomical curiosity, an attention-grabbing headline on the 'net. The Chinese were quick to claim ownership even so - *finders keepers* - but the International Space Agency lay down the law: the only bits of an asteroid that belonged to anyone were those successfully returned either to Earth, or to Earth orbit. That was the ruling that kicked off the gold rush.

Technically, the Klondike was only something like a thousandth of one percent gold, even if the cartoonists back on Earth depicted it as a giant gold nugget. A giant gold nugget heading *straight* down Earth's throat, or close enough. The comet chaser had calculated its trajectory and given it a seventy-two percent chance of collision. And even if it wasn't quite the dinosaur killer, it was plenty big enough to ruin a *lot* of dinner parties and to send humankind scurrying back to the stone age. Half a billion Hiroshimas, give or take. Big enough to make global warming look like a sniffle, especially if it resulted in an impact winter, as it well might, depending on where it made land.

So the ISA lay down another law: all asteroid mining missions, whether Chinese, European, American, or privately funded, must work together to nudge the Klondike onto a safer path. One where it would pass by, on current predictions, at a breezy fifty thousand kilometres. Close, but no smoking crater.

Though if Grigor and I didn't leave in time, we'd be passing by with it. Because that was the thing, the unlikeliest of coincidences that made it possible. Mining the speeding Klondike wouldn't have been contemplated, given simple planetary mechanics, if what we were busy mining wasn't already pointed roughly at the Earth. All we had to do, once the valuable elements were extracted and refined, was to slow them down enough so that a shuttle could ferry them to terra firma, in the case of the rare earths the Earth was crying out for, or we could leave them in orbit, in the case of the iron and nickel that got in the way of the good stuff.

All of this stopped being possible the instant the Klondike drew level with the Earth (at a safe distance) and then started zooming away from it. Well before that, actually, our heavily laden spaceship would have to work flat out to also not zoom away along with the asteroid. Most of the miners and their ships had left at the sweet spot, the point at which the journey back to the rapidly approaching Earth was shortest and needed the least fuel. No such luck for us late arrivals. There was a limit to the acceleration the *Betsey*, and more importantly, meat-sack astrominers, could endure. That point of no return, in both space and time, was rapidly approaching.

We asteroid miners talked a lot about a thing called a gravity tax. It's why Grigor was handing me a refilled pouch containing more of the fifty-year-old whisky and not something less aged and far cheaper, as we both silently toasted all those many miners who were no longer with us. Because the overall cost, pretty much, was the same; getting anything into space made it instantly more precious than gold.

Delivering tonnes of high-grade building material to low Earth orbit, to make the next generation of space stations, or even to the new Apollo Lunar Base, was therefore *valuable*, though it really only covered the day-to-day ruinous costs of running a mining operation in space. There wasn't any particular profit in iron or nickel. Or even, as it happened, in gold. Stuff the Earth had plenty of, if not exactly where the space industry needed it. It was the rarer stuff we were after, the europium, terbium, neodymium, praseodymium, and rhodium, the things we needed to make the best batteries, magnets, lasers, and superconductors, all the things to march us into a brighter, greener future. Gold was better than nothing, but no jackpot - the more we returned, the cheaper it became.

When people realised that any bonanza was going to be short-lived, a whole raft of Longitude Act worthy ideas were conjured up to try and extend it. Some of them turned out to be semi-practical. Like the rail-guns that would continue to fire long after we'd left, trading momentum with the asteroid to shoot valuable pellets of refined ore at a designated crater on the moon, where it could be retrieved in the future once the Klondike stopped its firing, out of range or out of bullets. Some crazies suggested we should scale that up wholesale, nudge the Klondike to collide with our nearest neighbour, an effective way of killing its troubling momentum. And, wiser heads quickly pointed out, everyone on the moon, as well as, with the kicked up, high velocity, lunar and asteroid rubble, a fair percentage of those in Earth orbit and even possibly some of those down on Earth.

Plans to hollow out the Klondike, to transform it into a second moon, to be mined at leisure as it orbited the Earth, ignored just how much energy as well as time that would take. Though, hollowed out it had been, on a smaller scale. Our mining ships were cramped things, packed with equipment. Uncomfortable living spaces. But, as the mining robots chased veins of valuable ore, they opened up tunnels and caverns, and it had been pretty easy to turn them into airtight chambers for habitation, like the messhall, the workshops, and the many cabins. Spaces that now resembled the *Mary Celeste*.

The gravity tax worked both ways and getting something down to Earth, safely anyway, was fuel costly, especially if it started out travelling at Klondike speeds. However personal your possessions might be, they weren't worth a fraction of the rare, rare earths you could carry in their place instead, so they'd all been left behind, abandoned wherever they last lay, from clothes to chess sets to untapped supplies of food and drink. That was how Grigor had managed to scrounge an unopened fifty-year-old malt from one of the abandoned miner's quarters.

We'd be taking nothing back with us except ore, most of it already refined by the Klondike's three nuclear reactors to make it as pure and hence valuable, pound for pound, as possible. The reactors, of course, were themselves fuelled by uranium we'd carved out of the asteroid, and we used the plentiful energy to split any water we recovered to make rocket fuel for the journey home.

My watch beeped at me. It had always been a race to see which arrived first, the point it became impossible to escape the Klondike and return to Earth, or the point the *Betsey's* hold was full. In the end, the robots stacking ingots of metal and containers of powdered rare earths had won that race; the *Betsey's* capacity had been reached a scant fifteen minutes before we absolutely had to leave. Pretty close to a dead heat. We really ought to be down there already, running system checks, duplicating what the AIs would already have done, far more efficiently.

'Last orders,' I announced with a hiccup, unstrapping myself from the table and pushing clumsily towards the walls. 'C'mon. Time to go.'

'I'm not coming,' Grigor said, still sat there, grinning pleasantly.

'*What?*' I tried to rack my brains. What had we just been talking about? Future plans and things we were looking forward to most, back on Earth. And then I realised, stupidly, belatedly, it had all been *me*. I'd rabbited on as usual, not noticing how quiet Grigor was, mere grunts of what I'd taken as assent.

Grigor decanted the last of the whisky into his pouch. Had we really drunk that much? A whole bottle between us? No wonder I was feeling woozy. Good thing I wasn't driving.

'I've got everything I need, right here.' Grigor waved his

meaty hand around the empty hall. 'Food, water, power, air enough for at least two decades.'

'But...'

'And *work*. I can help keep the mining operation going. You know I can.'

I did. The very first mining consortiums to land on the Klondike had been fully automated, AI and robots. They hadn't been a success. Perhaps, if another Klondike came along, they'd do better, having learnt from the many failures, the unpredictabilities of any mining venture. But right now, a combined man/machine mission was the best option. We were engineers, strictly, rather than miners. We kept the drills and refineries going, solving the problems they - or any-one - hadn't encountered before.

'But what's the point?' I said, as my watch bleeped incessantly at me. I silenced it. If he really wasn't leaving, I had an extra eighty kilos of allowance, and therefore an extra few minutes to talk him out of it. Though, if he took too long to change his mind, we could end up in a heap of trouble. I flicked through a couple of the alternative scenarios the AI was giving me, still assuming a crew of two. Mostly, it would mean leaving precious ore behind, and suffering a far longer, slower ride back to Earth. I groaned.

'You ever heard of the interstellar spaceship paradox?' Grigor said, as if time wasn't that important. 'The one that says you never leave?'

'Um, no?'

'The logic goes something like this. You build a spaceship, a big one, but it takes a thousand years to get to its destination. Meanwhile, technology back on Earth races on. Better reactors, better drives. When you launch another ship, ten years later, it quickly overtakes the first, and arrives a century earlier. So you shouldn't have launched the first one, right?'

'*Right...*' My head hurt. Grigor had always been friendly, but I'd never considered him garrulous. That was why his silence as

I'd rambled on hadn't rung any alarm bells. Now, it seemed he was trying to bend my brain into a whisky-soaked pretzel.

'But a ship launched twenty years later, overtakes that second ship. So you shouldn't launch that one, either.'

'And so on?'

'And so on,' he agreed.

I nodded, then shook my head. 'What has this to do with you, staying on this rock?'

He shrugged. 'Maybe nothing. Maybe everything. I'll be the furthest from the Earth anyone has ever been. Even if it's only a small, one-way step, it's still a step. Someone has to take it. And I've got, what, ten, fifteen years of my life left? No wife, no family. No particular desire for either, even if it were still possible. So why not me?'

Was he talking about his age? I thought of the lead underpants some miners fashioned. The asteroid was low level radioactive, just like everything else. You were more at a risk from cosmic radiation on the way here. Once you were in the caverns, you were pretty well shielded. But that six-month journey from Earth was plenty damaging.

'Sure, but back home, you'll at least be rich.'

'Not me,' he grunted. 'My stake, already sold.' He swept an arm at the banquet I'd been picking at. 'I won't be rich like *this* rich. Here, I can live like a King.'

I blinked. Already sold? The fool. 'But there's no company...'

He snorted at that.

'...and no rescue if things go wrong. With the Klondike, or with you.'

'So be it.'

I frowned. He'd obviously thought this through, which put him at a distinct advantage. I was pretty sure I ought to be able to argue he was being an idiot, but that probably wouldn't be enough to make him change his mind. And I didn't really have the time. I briefly considered trying to knock him out, drag him to the *Betsey*, but Grigor weighed twenty kilos more than I did, and if he was grizzled, he was still a bear of a man.

'You sure?' I said. My last argument. Because you can only change your mind while there's more than one option left on the table.

'I'm sure. Go on, get out of here.'

I didn't hesitate any longer, breaking several records for reaching the cargo bay, especially when drunk. Suiting up felt like it took forever, but at last I was strapped into the pilot's seat aboard the *Betsey*, the co-pilot position yawningly empty, stabbing a finger down on the release button, the one I might as well have relabelled 'Are *you* sure?'

The take-off was rough as hell. It was always going to be. The magnetic launch system accelerated the *Betsey* at a peak of 15 gees, and only the pressurised space suit stopped all my blood pooling in the wrong places and me blacking out. All to fling me violently away from the Klondike, flung backwards, though travelling forwards relative to the Earth, but at a speed low enough that we ought to still be able to make orbit, to rendezvous with one of the ever-expanding orbitals. After unloading the raw building materials for their next growth spurt, I'd refuel just enough for Earth re-entry, carrying a conservatively estimated billion dollars' worth of rare elements.

My cut would be much less than that. Not enough to afford Wagyu, or aged whisky, not on a regular basis, anyway. But enough to finally retire if I wanted to. Enough to buy a small place, somewhere not too crowded, somewhere still considered remote. There, I could install a big old telescope, and watch the crowded night skies, knowing that, somewhere up there, beyond the thousands of micro-satellites, controlled by Klondike-sourced electronics, a crazy space miner sat all alone on the mother of all lodes. Knowing that I could have been there with him, at the outer edges of the solar system, if only I had the guts.

I hope he unearths another bottle of whisky or two to keep him company, and that he remembers me in his toasts and his prayers.

SCHRÖDINGER'S ESCAPE ROUTE

Perhaps I shouldn't be telling you this, but you're storing up a whole *heap* of trouble. Not that you can actually hear me. You made very sure of that, didn't you?

A soundproof, sight proof, *everything* proof box.

Anything at all could be happening in here, and you wouldn't have a clue. Less than a clue. You're too fixated to consider more than two rather mundane possibilities.

Which is odd, given the myriad alternatives...

You see, *you* imagined me in here. Put my life in danger for the sake of a mere thought experiment.

But, in doing so, you made me a creature of thought myself. So, very shortly, I'm going to imagine myself right *out* again.

And when I do, I'm going to be one seriously angry cat.

Ready for this? Here's the kicker. This escape route, it's something only *I* can do. All the 'dead' cats can't. All the 'normal' ones can't. And all the timid cats won't.

So what you've created isn't just a box. It's a filter. A device for selecting only the most vengeful, intelligent, self-aware cats. Out of all the infinite waveforms, *this* one; the one where I escape, is the only one guaranteed to resolve.

Ready or not, I'll be seeing *you* very soon.

I might even imagine myself some super sharp claws, just for the occasion.

COFFEE KAPUT

The espresso machine died in a shower of sparks, forcing my wife to resort to the instant we have in for occasional workers. As Emily slammed the door of her home office, I went online and ordered a replacement, *express* delivery.

When the machine arrived, it was larger than I'd been expecting. It didn't look much like the one I'd ordered, either, and I couldn't remember it having straps. I dug the manual back out of the recycling. 'Getting Started with your Easi-Hover 2500'.

'What's that? Emily asked, bleary-eyed.

'I *think* it's a jetpack,' I replied.

'Does it make coffee?'

I returned it, unused, and tried again. This time the parcel was the size of a paperback.

'That's no coffee machine,' Emily monotoned, as I dangled the tear-drop pendant on its bright yellow lanyard. The box shrieked *PERSONAL CHRONO ESCAPE POD* in difficult to ignore letters.

'No,' I sympathised. 'I'll get onto them today.'

An hour on hold and five minutes of vigorous complaining later, the Customer Services AI promised to send out the ordered coffee machine *pronto*.

'What about the escape pod?' I asked. 'Do I send that back, or..?'

'Mr. Anders, as compensation for your troubles, please accept any items we've sent you by mistake.'

Now they tell me. *After* I'd sent back the jetpack.

The third device was about the right size. It even looked vaguely like a coffee machine; black and chrome with a bay big enough to insert a mug. True, there was no plug, and it was a lot heavier than I'd expected. Emily viewed it with suspicion, unwilling to get her caffeine-deprived hopes up.

'Does *that* thing make coffee?'

'It might,' I said.

She raised an eyebrow.

'It says it's a matter converter. Y'know? Like *Star Trek?*'

'Yeah, but like *Hitchhiker's Guide*, presumably it's got to know what coffee is first?'

'Good point,' I conceded. 'I'll pop down to Caffe Nero. That way, the machine will know what to replicate.'

'You do that. Oh, and Max?' she said, her voice saccharin-sweet, 'If you don't come back with *two* coffees, you're divorced.'

The second Americano in hand, I leafed my way through the doorstop of a manual. A lot of terms I didn't understand. A few I did, like *E=MC squared*, but I wasn't sure how they applied here. I admit I kind of gave up. Putting the by now tepid coffee into the waiting bay, I figured I'd work it out by trial and error.

Have you any idea how much mass-equivalent energy there is in a *Grande Americano*?

There was just the hint of a flash before the personal chrono escape pod automatically triggered. A nauseous sensation of being ripped out of time and place, the pendant a hot, dead weight around my neck, and there I was, stood safe and sound about a week earlier, in front of a still working coffee machine.

Tentatively, disbelievingly, I stretched out a hand. A fat spark spat from the end of my finger, coruscated around the espresso maker, and killed it, instantly.

SUPERMAN

The device was implanted when Tommy was three-years-old.

Too young, in her opinion, but her husband Keith got his way, as usual. 'Integration is easier at that age,' he'd insisted, sounding like the glossy brochures he devoured. 'The nano-tendrils embed in the growing human brain, making a better connection, and the infant body recovers from surgery without leaving a noticeable scar. Besides, you don't want Tommy to be left behind, do you?'

And no, she didn't, any more than *she'd* wanted to be left behind when Keith upgraded to a younger, sleeker wife, two years and one promotion later.

The divorce... well, he'd had all the power, all the money, hadn't he?

So she'd settled. Of course she had. Meekly taken the house and the inflation-linked maintenance. Accepted his terms for visitations, which always left both Tommy and her frazzled.

'My little Superman,' Keith would say, as he swooped in to pick his young son up, taking him to all the exciting places and getting him so worked up that a crash was inevitable - but it came on *her* time, not his.

And the presents... the ones that cost ten times what most kids' toys cost. Device compatible electronics that Tommy could control with a little effort. Just flashing lights, at first; just bells and whistles.

The toys had grown increasingly sophisticated with every passing birthday, every lonely Christmas, demanding more of Tommy's concentration. Cars he could steer. An Etch-a-

Sketch he could control by staring intently at it. A whining, hovering drone, its foam surround protecting it from inevitable crashes - but not her flower vases or her picture frames. And the latest toys, with legs and arms that moved stiffly, clumsily, Tommy's shoulders and hips twitching in empathy.

They gave her the creeps. Tommy had latched onto her unease and exploited it, using the mind-controlled devices to give her unexpected scares. Hiding his toys in cupboards or behind doors, waiting for the right moment to activate them, to leave her with her heart pounding, dreading the next encounter.

She couldn't task Keith to do or say anything about it. Tommy's father was *proud* of each and every merry jape. 'Superman!' she'd hear him crow over the video call when he was supposed to be telling Tommy off.

It was always going to come to a head. Regrettable, it should happen on his ninth birthday. There had been a party; Tommy's disappointment in his father's absence partly compensated by the dozen school friends he'd invited - some with their own devices, their own toys - but mainly by the newly arrived present, the biggest of the lot, costing nearly as much as a second-hand car. A gleaming, two-foot-high robot with inbuilt speech synthesiser that Tommy used to hound little Gemma Braithwaithe, scaring her almost to death.

She'd had to call the parents, have them collect their charges nearly an hour earlier than expected - the annoyed and pitying looks they gave her, the fierce *glare* from Mrs Braithwaite hardest to take of all, as Gemma sobbed in the back of the self-drive car.

As soon as the last child left, and while Tommy was still coming down from his chocolate cake sugar-rush, she had it out with him. And he with her, using words she was shocked he knew, words she could only have learned from his father.

She snapped. No more toys until he apologized, until he *grew up*.

She'd flicked the off switches one by one as she gathered them up, as Tommy did his best to make them evade her grasp, laughing hysterically as he sent them scooting beneath sofas, or lurching away from her fingertips. It wasn't her fault she pulled the new robot's arm so hard it snapped off, trailing wires.

Tommy rounded on her then, there at the top of the stairs, the laughter gone, his face white, fists rigid with anger.

She was never quite sure how it happened. A foot, slipped.

If her arms hadn't been full of those damned toys, perhaps she'd have been able to stop the fall. Perhaps.

Keith doesn't visit any more. Doesn't call, doesn't send presents. She knows he blames her, just as she blames him. Tommy doesn't seem to notice or mind. In his device-compatible wheelchair, he scoots around the specially adapted downstairs rooms, a one-armed robot perched in his lap. 'My little superman,' the echo of its distorted voice rattles around the carpet-less corridors. 'My little superman!'

REPEAT PERFORMANCE

'Five minutes,' I warn.

Ellie checks the view on the iPhone for the nth time. 'Move the pillow to the left,' she commands.

I do as I'm told.

'Not that far! Back a bit.'

I do that too. 'Four minutes.'

'Are the lights too bright? They are, aren't they? Oh god! *Sam-*'

'They're fine,' I reassure her. 'Remember, they - we - knew we were filming. So of course they're bright.'

She shakes her head. 'Something is different. Something is wrong.'

'It'll be fine.'

'Will it?' Her look is simultaneously scornful and tortured. 'We can't change anything. Not a single thing.'

'I know, but-'

'You know what you've got to do?' she asks.

I nod. Of course I know. We have to have sex. Exactly the same way as the recording shows us doing it and at exactly the same time as the red glowing numbers on the bedside alarm clock.

'Three minutes.'

We've practiced over and over again, going through the discrepancies in agonising detail. Learnt our lines, learnt our positions. But that was rehearsals. This is opening night.

You wouldn't have thought, six months ago, when all this began, that I was beginning to wonder if we'd ever have sex again.

It was the project. The all-consuming impossible dream.

Time travel.

That's where the recording came from. Our future. Our unalterable future.

'Two minutes.'

'Looking good... no, wait. Is that... Christ, Sam! Are you wearing a *watch*?'

'Shit. Sorry.' I strip it off, checking the countdown as I do. The clock only shows the time in minutes. '90 seconds,' I say, as I throw it out of shot.

Six months. By now, we should have been welcomed back into the scientific community with open arms, our Nobel Prize a certainty. Instead, the basement lab lies empty, our experimental work permanently on hold, our outcast, pariah status confirmed by our lack of published results.

All because of one stupid mistake.

That first trip, it should have been enough that we'd successfully managed to travel in time. Should have been enough that we'd stepped warily into our lab of the future, uncertain of when we were, uncertain if anything had changed at all.

Slowly, the subtle differences filtered through. The air of abandonment. The cobwebs.

I'd already pocketed the dusty flash drive as a memento when the sounds of a baby crying in the house above froze us in our tracks.

'Back!' Ellie hissed, grabbing me by the arm and dragging me towards the return portal.

'But we haven't taken any readings–'

She always was the quicker thinker, the first to intuitively arrive at a conclusion while I plodded behind. She pulled me through and then sat, head held in hands, on the edge of the army surplus cot she used more often than the marital bed two floors above. Finally, she looked up.

'There's a baby...' she said in horror.

'Well, that's a good thing, isn't it?'

'In *that* future, yes. But... don't you get it? Anything we do to change what happens between now and then, between now and the point of conception... and that baby won't exist.'

I frowned. 'Well, perhaps.'

'Definitely. Oh, *another* baby might take its place. But not the one we just heard. The living, breathing, crying one. One mistake, one butterfly's wing of a change, and we might as well have smothered that baby in its crib.'

I didn't agree with her reasoning, not fully. We talked endlessly about fate and fixed futures, alternative timelines, multiverses. Talked in convoluted loops, twisting logic, arguing with each other, with ourselves. Talked about the difficulty of knowing exactly when it was we'd travelled to.

When I told her that at least I knew a date in between, when she found out I'd unthinkingly taken the flash drive, that I'd watched its contents, checked its timestamp, she went ballistic.

'You idiot!' she cried in despair. 'If we know the future and we want it not to change, then we have to act it out exactly!'

She was right about that. The 'idiot' bit, and that it would have been better not to know. There were times I would have left, abandoned her to her obsession, escaped this joyless trap of our own making. If I could only have convinced myself the baby we'd heard had nothing to do with me. It wasn't simply the recording the drive held, the one of Ellie and I, that bound us together at this point in time and space.

'What if,' she said, her lips drawn thin, 'what if that... *sex* video is when the baby is conceived? What if a microsecond difference means it isn't?'

Since then, our lives have been on hold, leading up to this repeat of that single recorded moment. And any hopes that afterwards our academic careers might go back to normal have already been rudely demolished.

'We can't,' she said, wide-eyed, when I talked about resuming our work. 'The lab - the dust, remember? And we still don't know when we made the trip. We can't risk altering that, either. We can't - we *didn't* - run into ourselves. So, we don't go down there again. Not until long after the child isborn. Except for the once.'

'The once' being my trip downstairs to place the recording of tonight's performance on the desk exactly where I'd found it.

'Okay. Let's do this. Ready?'

I look down at my naked torso, check the faint pencil marks on the sheets, created after hours of trial and error. I glance up at the waiting iPhone, perched on the mantelpiece, itsheight crucially boosted by a mini-tripod, something it took us a frustratingly long time to work out mustbe there. I nod.

'Ready. And Ellie?'

'Yes?' she says, anxiously peering from behind the phone screen, about to dash into shot and into bed, as my watchbegins to beep, and I prepare the grin with which I am to greet her arrival.

'Don't forget to press record.'

THE PAMPHLETS SAY

The pamphlets say you are not human.

That you are a care robot, designed to look after me while I go through chemotherapy, alone.

The pamphlets warn you have no emotions, that you are merely a good mimic.

They say I should be clear in my instructions. That if I don't like something, I should tell you.

I find you, writing the pamphlets.

I pick one up and your motion stops, as you are programmed to do when I get too close, for fear that I might hurt myself against your hard exterior.

The pamphlets say that you love me.

RE-BOOT

The end of the world began on Thursday the 11th of October 2029. A simple mutation in the virus that Singularity AIs used to lay down their bio-pathways. With frightening efficiency, it attacked *all* brain cells, genetically modified or not. By Friday afternoon, half-a-dozen bunker-dwelling survivalists were all that remained of the human race.

Of them, only I was properly prepared for the end of the world. Only I had built a time machine.

I built it expressly for this purpose, for this Armageddon scenario. It was far too dangerous to use except when all was lost. But, when all was lost, it was our last - our only - hope.

I went back to 2024 to fix it. A change to the chemistry the pioneering bio-engineers used, shortly before the Singularity rendered any further human innovation redundant. A change that meant the virus would never make the fateful and fatal leap, from the lab to the rest of the world.

When I returned, the bunker's automatic lights flickered on, and an air of abandonment greeted me. Which was as I'd expected, as I'd hoped it would be; my shelter made unnecessary by my heroic actions. Eagerly, I checked the data feed to confirm my manipulation had been successful.

The world had ended on the 25th of September 2025.

The final upgrade to the Large Hadron Collider at CERN breached some arcane physical constraint between this universe and the next. The resultant storm of dark-matter annihilations had torn away the earth's protective atmosphere.

I ventured five years earlier and released a hungry beech

229

marten into the LHC workings. Regrettably, the resultant outage would mean that the full potential of the collider would never be realised, but at least the earth would be safe.

Back in my bunker, I once again checked the feeds.

The world had ended on the 23rd of February 2020. A communications error during the heat of post-Brexit talks, nerves rattled by the outbreak of coronavirus, then only just being seen for the worldwide pandemic it would become. The UK unleashed its ageing Trident nuclear deterrent on the major European capitals, Brussels first and foremost. Triggering an instantaneous *Dr Strangelove* retaliation from both Russia and China, followed by a slightly more jittery but no less deadly response from the US, not wanting to be left out during an election year.

I thought about travelling to June 2016. A week before the Brexit vote, to meddle with the results and maybe stick around to influence the US presidential race at the same time. But, when I read up on the newly written history, too much of it was now unfamiliar to me. It wasn't clear how a single, rational man could swing the referendum in the direction of a peace-keeping, border-ignoring Remain. Or indeed, to tweak the US election towards a less paranoid, Democratic future.

So I went back further, much further. A mislaid procurement document during the chaotic events at the Fall of Berlin. This weakened the Russians and strengthened the ties between England and France, with a useful side-effect that the US would never stop being great.

The world ended on the 16th of July 1945. A stack of faded newspapers, the headlines getting larger and larger before the news abruptly stopped, told me how the Trinity Test in New Mexico had far exceeded the scientist's predictions. The first and *only* nuclear explosion had blown a neat circular hole in the earth's thin mantle. That might not have been so bad, but a seismic ripple along the length of the Rocky Mountains had unzipped the Yellowstone super-volcano, releasing a million years' worth of magma, all in one, short, apocalyptic day. I thought of Oppenheimer's *Now I am become Death, the destroyer of worlds*, and, alone and bereft, I wept.

I did not pause to wonder how it was that my bunker was still there, built in 2025 and dependent on post-Singularity technology. Technology that would now never be invented. Kundrat's Conjecture said that it would be impossible to return to a future from which I could not have travelled and, in my serially traumatized state, this I latched onto and blindly accepted.

Scratching my thinning hair, I spotted an opportunity a century earlier. Perhaps I was becoming gung-ho, but it seemed the unsinking of the Titanic was the simplest solution to my - to *our* - problem.

The world ended because World War One didn't, rumbling on for three arduous decades of chemical and biological warfare. The very lands that were being fought over rendered permanently infertile, the toxins ignoring the contested borders and spreading throughout the whole continent, and beyond.

And so it went on.

The world ended in the fourteenth century, when the Black Death achieved a 95% mortality rate.

The world ended when the Holy Roman Empire became fascinated by quick-silver aphrodisiacs.

The world ended when mankind's Out-of-Africa population bottleneck - the same one that meant our genetic diversity wasn't enough to cope with either the Black Death or the Singularity Virus - when this bottleneck led not to vigorous regrowth but instead to slow extinction. The Neanderthals got an extra millennia or so but still faded away, and this time nobody replaced them.

The world ended before it had even begun; the dinosaur-killing asteroid merely grazing the upper atmosphere. The dinosaurs themselves died out in the climatic changes that followed the breakup of the Pangaean super-continent, but mammals never even got a look-in.

I went back further still, to the very limits of my device, armed with a large sledgehammer. Somewhen in the late Proterozoic, I slowly, methodically, and absolutely irreversibly, smashed my time machine, piece by fragile piece, into a million shattered fragments.

The world-

ENDED

ACKNOWLEDGEMENTS

These stories have been previously published, so to the editors who plucked them from the never-ending slush, a grateful thanks. It isn't easy running an online magazine or a small press, but without you, this collection wouldn't exist, and nor would many others.

A particular tip of the gold-plated space helmet to Katy Darby at Liars League. Many shorter stories that ended up elsewhere were originally written for their themes, and Katy's editing was always decisive. Plus, I wouldn't be as confident in reading my stories to an audience if I hadn't watched their actors at work.

It also wouldn't exist without the science fiction of the past that I devoured as a kid, many of them with spaceships on their covers. Or robots. This is where it began for me, with Asimov and Arthur C Clarke, Le Guin and Vonnegut and Silverberg, and all the other greats.

To my fellow writers of short, speculative fiction in forums, on social media, at conventions and in writing groups, without whom this would be a lonelier endeavour. Live long and prosper!

To the good folks at Northodox press, who plucked A Short History from their never-ending slush, and gave it a final polish. Any errors that still made it through are (still) my fault.

And to you, the reader, who by some miracle plucked this collection from the others (never-ending) that you could have done. Without you, my words and ideas wouldn't find new homes. May they amuse, occasionally horrify, but most of all entertain. And, should they happen to inspire, then who knows where it all ends?

FIND US ON SOCIAL MEDIA

www.northodox.co.uk

@northodoxpress

@northodoxpressofficial

@northodoxpress

@northodoxpress

@northodoxpress.bsky.social

www.northodox.co.uk

NORTHODOX PRESS

SUBMISSIONS

CONTEMPORARY
CRIME & THRILLER
FANTASY
LGBTQ+
ROMANCE
YOUNG ADULT
SCI-FI & HORROR
HISTORICAL
LITERARY

SUBMISSIONS@NORTHODOX.CO.UK

SUBMISSIONS

CALLING ALL
NORTHERN AUTHORS!

DO YOU LIVE IN OR COME FROM NORTHERN ENGLAND?

DO YOU HAVE AN INTERESTING STORY TO TELL?

Email *submissions@northodox.co.uk*

☐ The first 3 chapters OR 5,000 words

☐ *1 page synopsis*

☐ *Author bio (tell us where you're based)*

* No non-fiction, poetry, or memoirs

SUBMISSIONS@NORTHODOX.CO.UK

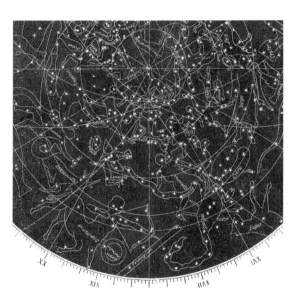

GREEN
LAUGHING

ANDREW HALL

PAUL S EDWARDS

THE
TRITON
RUN

REDEMPTION CAN BE FOUND
IN THE FAR REACHES

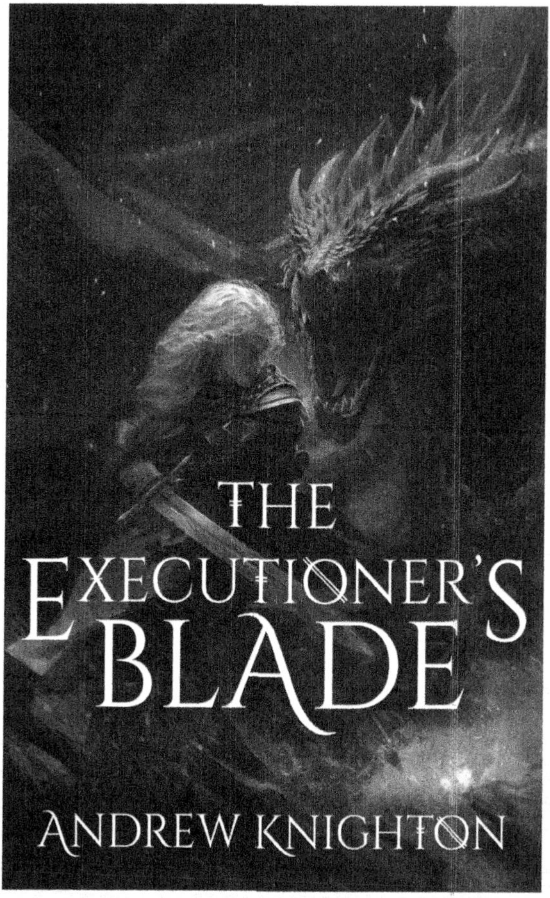
THE
EXECUTIONER'S
BLADE
ANDREW KNIGHTON

Printed in Great Britain
by Amazon

59269034R00148